Summer Scan

Susanne McCarthy

ISBN-13: 978-1724074935

Annis remembered Theo Lander. When she was sixteen, all the girls in her class used to sigh over him, giggling as they walked home from school past his father's garage, where he worked. Then his father had gone to prison, and Theo had left town.

So what was he doing back here now, nine years later, at her father's funeral?

Theo remembered George Statham's spoiled daughter, with her haughty, high-flown ways. Did she have any idea that her world was about to come crashing down around her? Because Theo had turned the tables on George Statham – and now he owned everything she had thought was hers.

So maybe it would be interesting to stick around after all.

TABLE OF CONTENTS

CHAPTER ONE

"DAMMIT – what the devil's *he* doing here?"

Annis glanced up, startled by Uncle Charles's uncharacteristic outburst. "Who?" Her fine violet-blue eyes scanning over the politely sombre company as they strolled back through the rain towards the line of cars parked on the cemetery's gravel path.

She knew everyone here. None of them were really what you could call friends of her father – a handful of business associates, a few acquaintances from the golf club, here for form's sake as much as anything.

Everyone, except…

"Lander." Uncle Charles muttered the name as if it was a bad taste in his mouth. "I thought we'd seen the last of him nine years ago."

Annis frowned. The name did ring a bell.

"You'll be too young to remember, of course. He used to live around here at one time. Bad family – father went to prison." Uncle Charles had taken her arm, holding his big black umbrella over both of them as he steered her firmly towards the front car. "If you take my advice, my dear, you'll have nothing at all to do with him."

Theo Lander. Yes, she remembered. She remembered very well.

It had been quite a scandal for the respectable little Yorkshire town. But though the name may have slipped back into the mists of half-forgotten memory, the man standing a little apart from the rest of the mourners, apparently reading the cards attached to the impressive display of wreaths, would never fade so obligingly away.

Nine years ago. She had been sixteen, and Theo would have been… oh, somewhere in his early twenties, perhaps. All the girls in her class used to sigh over him, engraving his name in the back of their exercise books, giggling as they walked home from school past his father's garage, where he worked.

5

In an old T-shirt, stained with oil and stretched taut across his wide shoulders, and a pair of faded jeans which fitted him as if he had been born in them, he was like a magnet for a clutch of silly schoolgirls – all the more of an attraction, perhaps, because he had virtually ignored them.

The other lads who worked in the garage would grin, and try to flirt with them, but they weren't nearly so interesting. It was Theo Lander, leaning over an engine bay or wiping his hands on a piece of old rag, whose notice they had craved and competed over.

And oh, the thrill of those rare occasions when he did spare a fleeting glance in their direction – those dark, dangerous eyes, that blue-black hair curling over the nape of his neck, long enough to be an affront to every anxious parent who had deplored his disruptive effect on their not-so-innocent daughters. Dynamite!

He hadn't changed much, Annis noted, studying him covertly from behind the fine black veil which covered her eyes. His hair was cut rather shorter now, but that had done little to civilise him. Nor had the well-cut black cashmere overcoat he was wearing. Even from this distance she could recognise its quality.

He must have done pretty well for himself since he had left Ridgely, she reflected dispassionately, in spite of the scandal which had sent his father to prison. But there was still that intriguing hint of danger about him.

She became aware that he was watching her, and was suddenly glad that she had chosen to wear a hat with a veil, though it had seemed a little over-the-top when she had first tried it on. He was still standing by himself, one hand thrust deep into the pocket of his overcoat, apparently oblivious to the curious stares and covert whispers his presence had aroused.

For one long moment he held her gaze, and she felt an odd little flutter in the pit of her stomach. Dammit, he shouldn't be looking at her like that, as if the slimly-tailored lines of the black silk suit she was wearing revealed rather too much of her slender curves. This was her father's funeral, for goodness' sake!

With an effort of will, she managed to drag her eyes away, but not before she had noted the faintly mocking smile that curved that hard mouth. Yet surely from this distance, and through the shadow of her veil, he couldn't see the betraying hint of colour in her cheeks, nor even know that she was looking in his direction?

But even so, she was conscious that her heart was beating rather too fast. It was ridiculous to let herself react to him like that, she scolded herself impatiently. She was no longer a naïve young schoolgirl, her head stuffed full of romantic nonsense. She was twenty-five years old, and quite accustomed to having men stare at her – and more than capable of dealing with them, too.

Their progress to the car was hampered by people who wanted to shake Annis's hand and say a few conventional words of condolence. "I'm so sorry, my dear. Such a shock for you. But at least it was quick – better than if he had suffered a long illness."

What were you supposed to say under such circumstances? For once she was glad of Uncle Charles's interfering presence as he responded for her, deftly moving each person along after a polite exchange of platitudes.

"Thank you. You will come back to the house? Oh, Gerald, a moment, if you have the time – those damned ramblers are demanding we open up that footpath again..."

"Miss Statham?"

She turned sharply. Theo Lander had finished studying the wreaths, and had chosen the exact moment when Uncle Charles was distracted to approach her – not by chance, she was quite sure.

At closer range, she could see the small differences that the years had wrought – a hint of hardness around the mouth which as a teenager she had found so intriguing, matched by a hardness in those dark, level eyes.

That well-cut overcoat, and the expensive patina on his hand-stitched black leather shoes, suggested a discreet aura of wealth – but she didn't think she'd care to speculate on just how that wealth had been acquired.

"Mr.Lander." Somehow she managed to keep her voice cool as she extended a gloved hand in polite greeting.

He accepted her handshake, one dark, level eyebrow arched in question. "You remember me then?"

"Uncle Charles reminded me who you were," she was pleased to be able to retort with some truth, withdrawing her hand from his.

"Ah – of course." That hard mouth curved into a smile of sardonic amusement. "Now I believe I'm supposed to say something about regretting that the occasion of our meeting again should be one of such tragic sorrow."

"I really hope you won't!"

"Indeed I won't. I know you wouldn't believe any expression of grief on my part. And I can only admire the way you're maintaining your composure. That fetching little veil really doesn't quite conceal the fact that you haven't shed a single tear."

She flashed him an icy glare. It was quite true, of course – her eyes weren't even moist. At her mother's funeral, six years ago, she had cried so much she had thought her heart was being torn out.

But that had been her mother. Now, she would only have cried because it was expected that you should weep at your father's funeral - and she had never been the sort to play those kind of games.

"Lander." Uncle Charles's brusque voice saved her from the necessity of having to think of a response.

"Sir Charles." That cool gaze was transferred as he held out his hand again. "I'm pleased to meet you. I understand that you're one of the executors of Statham's will?"

"I am." A little to Annis's surprise, the older man refused the proffered hand. "But I fail to see that it's any business of yours."

"Oh, it's very much my business." That smile had an edge of sharpened steel. Theo slipped his hand into the inside pocket of his coat and drew out a discreetly embossed business card. "You can contact me on any of these numbers. I shall be expecting your call."

And slanting another enigmatic glance at Annis, which flickered down over her slender curves in a way that set her hackles bristling, he turned and strolled casually away towards the line of cars.

"Huh!" Uncle Charles expressed a snort of disgust. "Damned mongrel. Well, he needn't think he can come lording it around here. He may have a bit of money in his pocket now, but he's still nothing more than a second hand car salesman."

Theo Lander ignored the falling rain, watching as the last of the funeral cars drew away. So this was the end, he reflected darkly. The final curtain. Was that why he had chosen to come? To witness the closing act of the play, on behalf of his father?

Should he feel some kind of remorse? If he had known that George Statham had heart problems, would it have made any difference? Beneath his well-cut overcoat, his wide shoulders moved in a small shrug. It was immaterial now.

And besides, he reminded himself bitterly, Statham had shown his father not an ounce of compassion. Those dark eyes glittered with a fierce light. What goes around comes around.

And then there was the girl. He had to admit, there had been a certain curiosity. She had grown up into quite a beauty, he reflected as he walked back towards his own car, parked just inside the cemetery gates. The coltish legginess he remembered had matured into some very interesting curves, which the cut of that rather chic black silk suit had done nothing to disguise.

A small, secret smile curved that hard mouth as he opened the door of his sleek dark green Aston Martin and swung himself in behind the leather steering wheel. She had twisted her hair up into some kind of complicated knot beneath that frivolous little hat, with its nonsensical veil, but one glimpse had told him it was still the same rich-girl honey-gold colour he remembered from the days when he used to see her flouncing around the town as if she owned it.

And from the way she held herself, the way she had looked down her well-bred nose at him as she had shaken his hand, she still believed she was the Queen of the World.

That impression was borne out by the contents of the buff folder which right now was safely locked up in his desk drawer. The firm he had hired several years ago to supply him with press-clippings about George Statham had interpreted their brief rather widely, and had included snippets about the daughter – though culled from the gossipy type of women's magazines, rather than the financial pages.

It was exactly the kind of lifestyle he would have expected of Statham's spoiled little princess, he mused with some contempt. The typical rich-girl career of shopping and lunching with her friends between flashy society parties - no doubt that had been much too absorbing to allow time for anything as mundane as a job.

He knew the type well – there had been plenty of them these past few years. Beautiful parasites, who wouldn't have spared him a second glance in the days when his pockets weren't so well-lined.

Yes, he remembered the Statham girl, with her haughty, high-flown ways. Did she have any idea what was coming to her now? He found himself rather hoping that she didn't. He wanted to see the look on that lovely face when her world came crashing down around her.

Something stirred inside him – something not quite appropriate to the solemn occasion - and he smiled in grim amusement. Maybe this wasn't quite the final curtain after all.

♥

"He's looking a lot better. You've worked wonders with him."

The big grey horse slanted the whites of his eyes towards the vet, his slender neck quivering as Annis stroked her hand down its length. "Poor Silver," she murmured softly.

"He's had such a hard time. It would be lovely to find a new home for him, where they'll give him the care he deserves."

Vicky smiled, but shook her head. "It won't be easy. He's such a big horse to handle, and he's still very nervous."

Annis was forced to agree. The grey looked a different animal from the one who had arrived, thin and trembling, in her stable-yard just a few months before, but he still shied at the slightest alarm, and he hated loud noises. A shadow darkened her violet-blue eyes. She could only guess at the kind of experiences he must have endured before he had been rescued from his former home.

"Ah well." She laughed wryly as she slipped off his head-collar to let him run loose in the paddock. "If we can't find anywhere else for him, he can always stay here. One more permanent resident won't make that much difference."

With a lithe movement she swung herself up to perch on the top of the five bar gate to watch as the horse cantered down the slope to where the others peacefully cropped the lush green grass.

Cleo, with her foal, all gangly legs as he clung to his mother's side – both of them lucky to be alive after she had been left to starve in an abandoned horsebox in a lay-by on the A170; Dolly and Polly, two elderly donkeys who had been made redundant after many patient years of trudging the sands of a sea-side resort giving rides to hoards of excited children; Benji, Patches…

What had started out seven years ago as just helping out the local Horse Rescue Society by taking in one neglected donkey had somehow escalated. That first sad little waif called Fred, adopted as a companion for her own beloved Fergal, had been joined by a floating population of a dozen or so horses and donkeys who lived in the rambling stables at the back of the house, or enjoyed the sunshine in one of the two large paddocks which sloped down to the river.

And besides fostering them, she had found that she had a real knack for understanding whatever was needed to restore a frightened horse's confidence, to give it back its trust in people.

It was wonderful to see an animal which had arrived half-starved or ill-treated finally be ready for the day when a carefully selected family would come to collect it, and she would wave a bittersweet goodbye as yet another horse-box disappeared down the lane.

Vicky leaned her arms on the top bar of the gate beside her. "So – how did the funeral go?" she enquired with restrained sympathy. She was aware, though they had never directly discussed it, that the relationship between Annis and her father hadn't been close.

Annis shrugged, her slim shoulders a little tense. "Oh, pretty much how I'd expected. All the usual suspects, tricked out in their best black, mouthing all the usual platitudes. Oh, there was one surprise." Even as she said it she was wondering why she was bothering to mention it. "Theo Lander was there. Remember him?"

Vicky's eyes widened, and she whistled softly. "*Do* I? What's he doing back here? Is he still as handsome as the devil?"

Annis laughed, hoping her friend wouldn't notice anything forced in her airy unconcern. "The answer to the first question is, I haven't a clue. As to the second – well, yes, I suppose so." The memory of those dark, disturbing eyes rose vividly in her mind, but she pushed it resolutely aside. "He looked as if he's done quite well for himself, anyway. At least he wasn't wearing those dreadful oil-stained jeans he used to wear."

"I remember." The other girl sighed. "And we all used to drool over the way they clung around his backside. Men like that ought to be against the law. How any of us managed to pass our A levels, when we spent all our time looking for excuses to walk past his father's garage just to get a peek at him, I don't know!"

Annis laughed, perhaps a little too brightly. "He must have got quite fed up with it, an endless processions of love-struck school-girls gawking at him every day. No wonder he moved away!"

She skipped down from the gate, walking with her friend up through the cobbled stable-yard behind the house. A light breeze was tugging at her hair, and she pushed a few wayward strands back off her face.

It was a beautiful spring morning, sparkling fresh after yesterday's rain. She had been up early, as usual, galloping Fergal up over the sheep-cropped hillside above the town – in spite of the demands of the other horses, she always made some time each day just for him.

And a good gallop had been just what she had needed, to chase away the cobwebs. She had slept badly, troubled by fragments of dreams – dreams of a man with dark, dangerous eyes.

"I wonder if he'll stay around, now he's back?" Vicky mused as they reached her car.

Annis kept a carefully blank expression on her face. "Who?"

Vicky laughed. "The cat's mother – who do you think? Theo Lander, of course. That would make life a little more interesting."

"Victoria Bateman! You're a respectable married woman!"

"So?" The other girl chuckled. "That doesn't mean I can't look, does it? And from what I recall, Theo Lander was certainly worth looking at."

Annis had just let herself into the scullery behind the kitchen, and was tugging off her riding boots, when her phone rang. Standing with one boot in her hand, the other still on her foot, she pulled it from her pocket.

"Annis?"

"Oh... Yes, hi Uncle Charles." Why that odd little stab of disappointment? Who had she been hoping might call?

"Look, I'm afraid a bit of a problem has cropped up." The voice on the other end of the line sounded oddly constrained. For one fanciful moment, Annis was reminded of a film she had seen recently, where one of the characters had been talking on the phone while someone held a gun to his head.

"There appears to be some kind of… irregularity in your father's affairs."

"Irregularity?" She frowned. "What sort of irregularity?"

"It isn't something that I can explain on the telephone." He paused, seeming to need a moment to compose himself. Annis was puzzled. She had never known Uncle Charles to be anything less than supremely confident and in control. "I'm at your father's office now. Can you come over?"

"What, right now?" The note of urgency in his voice had stirred her sense of unease. "I've only just come in from the stables. I haven't even had breakfast yet."

"I think you should come at once."

She hesitated. A problem with her father's business affairs? That could be a bit of a nuisance. And it sounded pretty serious – it wasn't like Uncle Charles to get his feathers ruffled over nothing. "OK, I'll be there in about half-an-hour."

In fact it took her fractionally over twenty-five minutes. She had grabbed a banana and a glass of milk, had a quick wash at the sink instead of her usual shower, and changed at top speed into a tan faux-suede skirt and a cream silk shirt, a brass-link belt slung low around her waist. She had brushed her hair vigorously and caught it back loosely in a scrunchy, and slicked on some mascara and a pale coffee shade of lipstick.

Uncle Charles would probably complain that her skirt was too short, she reflected with a touch of wry amusement, but it was perfectly decent.

It wasn't far to the smart red-brick offices of G.C.Statham (Holdings) Ltd. Her father had developed the business campus on the fringes of the town himself, and naturally had reserved the prime spot for his own company. Turning off the roundabout and into the landscaped car-park, she drove straight down to her father's reserved space next to the wide front steps.

But it was already occupied. A brutish-looking Aston Martin, gleaming dark green, with a long curved bonnet over an engine that would leave her nippy little red sports-car standing…

Who owned a car like that? Someone who thought it entitled him to park wherever he damned-well pleased, apparently!

Uncle Charles's sedate BMW was parked beside it, which meant that she was forced to drive right over to the far side of the car-park and squeeze in next to a row of bollards. The space was so narrow that she had to slither out with the door just half-open – a manoeuvre which caused her short skirt to ride even further up her slim thighs.

She smoothed it down quickly, slanting a swift glance around - an odd prickly sensation at the back of her neck warned her that someone was watching her. But there seemed to be no-one around, so shrugging the moment aside, she swung her handbag onto her shoulder and walked smartly back to the wide glass front entrance.

Jill, the pretty blonde receptionist, glanced up as the automatic doors whispered open, greeting her with a slightly uncertain smile. "Ah… Annis. Er… Good morning."

She returned the smile reassuringly, aware that people were likely to be a little nervous about what to say to her – whether to mention her recent bereavement. "Hi Jill. I've just popped in to meet with my Uncle. I gather he's in my father's office?"

"Yes, of course." The girl seemed a little flustered as she picked up the telephone. "I'll let them know you're here."

"It's all right," Annis responded blithely. "He knows I'm coming – I'll just go right on up."

The lift arrived just as she reached it, and she stepped aside to let the people inside come out. A couple of them slanted her the same kind of quick, awkward smile the receptionist had, and moved quickly away. Slightly bemused, she stepped into the lift and pressed the button for the third floor.

As the door slid shut behind her, a sudden thought struck her. Jill had said 'them'. Who was with her Uncle?

The executive corridor was carpeted with a thick maroon plush-pile carpet which deadened every sound. Annis had always thought the place was a little too ostentatious, with those heavy Victorian hunting prints in their gilded frames hanging on the wood-panelled walls - as if it was trying to emulate some imposing London banking house.

If she didn't just sell the whole Company straight off, she would certainly get rid of those things.

The door at the far end of the corridor stood ajar, and she pushed it open without bothering to knock. Maggie, her father's secretary, was kneeling beside a filing cabinet, her arms already full of files. She glanced up quickly as Annis entered, several of the files slipping from her grasp. "Oh... Annis – you're here."

"So it seems." She laughed, again a little bemused. What was wrong with everyone today? Even the impeccably efficient Maggie seemed to be in a flap. "Here, let me give you a hand with those." She dropped easily to her knees, reaching to gather up the scattered files. "I suppose everything's a bit hay-wire at the moment?"

"Yes, it is. That is…"

The door opened behind her. Turning to look over her shoulder, she saw a pair of hand-made shoes in expensive-looking soft black leather, then a pair of light-grey suit-trousers with a crisply-pressed crease.

Tilting her head to look higher, she came to an immaculately tailored jacket, worn casually open over a fine white cotton shirt. No tie, the collar loosely unfastened to give a glimpse of a smattering of crisp dark curling hair…

"Well… Good morning, Miss Statham. What a pleasure to see you again."

That voice, low and slightly husky, held a note of sardonic amusement as his eyes dwelt on the picture she presented – kneeling at his feet, her short skirt exposing far too much of her slender thighs. And the direction of his lingering gaze left no doubt of the precise source of his pleasure.

She uttered a choking sound, dropping the files she had collected, and struggled awkwardly to stand up. "Wh… What are you doing here?" she demanded, furiously aware of the faint blush of pink that had risen to her cheeks. "This is my father's office."

"Ah." Theo Lander smiled that predator's smile, all formal politeness as he put his hand beneath her elbow to help her to her feet. "That's the point we invited you here to discuss. Can I offer you a coffee? Thank you, Maggie." He nodded the instruction to her father's secretary – *her father's* secretary – and held the door open for her to precede him through.

She shook his hand from her arm, trying not to notice the sizzling heat that was spreading from where he had touched her. The room was so familiar – the wood-panelled walls, the leather chesterfield sofas, the huge mahogany desk which her father had always felt lent him a certain air of *gravitas*.

But now Theo Lander had strolled around the desk to settle himself in her father's leather executive chair, as if he owned the place. She stared from him to Uncle Charles, who was sitting a little stiffly in the corner of one of the chesterfields, and back. "What's going on?" she demanded. "That's my father's desk. How dare you…?"

"Of course – you're curious to know what's happening." His voice was as smooth as polished steel – the voice of a man who was accustomed to being in control. "Perhaps your Uncle had better explain."

"Damn you, Lander." The older man was all angry bluster. "I don't know how you've managed to pull this off, but I'm quite sure there's something shady about it. Very shady indeed."

"Shady?" Theo was leaning back in the big leather chair, his arrogant head tilted against one of its wings, a predatory smile curving his hard mouth - a warning to anyone who might be deceived by that easy, laid-back manner that this was not a man to cross swords with. "You mean criminal?"

"Yes! If you want the word without the dressing on it – I do mean criminal." Uncle Charles ground out the words, almost shaking with anger. "Like father, like son – that's what I say. It's in the blood."

Annis was shocked by the virulence of the old man's words, but Theo Lander appeared to be merely amused by them. "Oh no – there was nothing criminal. You may have it investigated, if you wish."

"I shall. Oh yes, I most certainly shall." He prodded an aggressive finger towards the younger man. "Believe me, I have no intention of letting you get away with this." He marched over to the door, pausing with his hand on the knob. "Annis, my dear, I think you'd better come with me," he added, recovering his customary dignity. "I don't care to leave you alone with this… this…"

Theo arched one dark, level eyebrow in provocative question. "What exactly do you think I'm going to do to her, here in this office, with Maggie on the other side of the door?"

The older man looked as if he was about to blow a gasket.

"It's all right, Uncle Charles." Annis injected her voice with a note of cool assurance she was far from feeling. "You go. I'm not the least bit afraid of Mr.Lander." To emphasise the point, she sat down in one of the deep sofas, neatly crossing her legs at the ankle, folding her hands in her lap, the picture of composed elegance.

From the corner of her eye she saw Theo's smile of mocking appreciation, and tilted up her chin at a haughty angle. Whatever was going on, she had no intention of letting Theo Lander think he could hold the upper hand - years of standing up to her father in one of his tempers had taught her not to be easily intimidated.

Uncle Charles hesitated, uncertain, then with a snort of disgust he snatched open the door – almost colliding in the doorway with Maggie, who was carrying a small tray with three coffee cups and a plate of chocolate biscuits.

"Oh… I'm sorry."

She glanced up at him in astonishment as he stormed past her without a word of apology, startled by such uncharacteristic behaviour from one whom she had always known as a gentleman of the old school. She just managed to avoid spilling the tray, though a little coffee slopped into one of the saucers.

"Oh dear – I'll just get a couple of paper towels to mop that up. I brought another cup for you as well, Theo." She set the tray down on a corner of the large desk. "You've been so busy all morning."

"Thank you, Maggie." He slanted the secretary a disarming smile. "That will be all for now. But perhaps you could ask the senior managers to meet with me in the Board Room in one hour?"

"Of course."

Annis watched this pleasant interchange with mild disgust. So Theo Lander could turn on the charm when it suited him, she reflected acidly. Well, it may have worked on her father's gullible secretary, but it wasn't going to work on her. All her defences were bristling as Maggie left the room.

"So - would you mind telling me what exactly is going on?" she enquired, her voice tinged with frost.

He turned that smile on her, though Annis noticed that its quality had subtly changed. "Certainly." He took his coffee and sipped it, watching her with that disconcertingly level gaze. "How much do you know about your father's business affairs?"

She shook her head. "Not very much." He had never wanted her to. It had always annoyed her slightly that he had never been willing to let her take an interest in the company – she had always suspected that it might have been different if she had been a son.

In fact there had been several occasions these past couple of years when she had sensed that he had worries of some kind. But he had dismissed any questions with impatience, so she had stopped bothering to ask.

Besides, she had never dreamed that she would be forced to have anything to do with it for many years to come.

Theo was watching her, one dark eyebrow raised in sardonic amusement. "Your only interest was in spending the money?" he taunted.

"You can't say that." Her eyes flashed sparks of blue fire. "You know nothing about me."

Theo laughed dryly. "As it happens, I know quite a lot about you." With a lazy movement he picked up a buff folder from the pile on his desk and pushed it towards her.

She regarded it with suspicion. "What's this?"

"Open it and see."

The first sheet appeared to be some kind of report, with the logo of a private investigation company on the top. Her eyes widened. "You had me *investigated*?" she protested, shocked.

"I had your father investigated. The company interpreted their brief rather more widely than I had intended. It was a few years ago…"

"So I see…" Attached to the report were several sheets of pictures – clippings from gossip magazines, paparazzi shots snipped from various tabloid newspapers, all neatly labelled with source, date and location. She stared at the first one, and a bubble of laughter rose to her lips. "Oh, I remember that night. Some fancy charity thing my cousins dragged me to – all Lord This and the Countess of That doing their bit to save the rainforest or whatever. It was the most boring smug-fest I've ever attended – and my shoes were killing me all night!"

She flipped over a couple more. With her cousins again, leaving some trendy London nightclub – in some of them she did look a little tipsy, caught like a rabbit in the white glare of the photographers' flashbulbs. "Oh no – that one's awful!" she protested. "It makes me look like Quasimodo!"

"Hardly."

She tossed the file back on his desk. "So?" Her voice was heavily laced with acid. "You're going to base your opinion of me on a handful of old photos? Well, think what you like. I really couldn't give that." She snapped her fingers in a gesture of contempt.

"The point is that if you'd taken a little more interest, you might have been aware that your father had been over-extending himself these past few years."

"Really?" She re-crossed her legs, quite deliberately letting him catch a glimpse of her long, slender thighs. She was satisfied to see the flicker of interest in his eyes. *Oh yes, you can look, buddy, but there's no way you're ever going to touch.*

"Some years ago he let himself be drawn into a rather unwise bidding war for a large patch of land near Leeds. It had outline planning permission for light industrial development, good motorway access – potentially a very valuable acquisition."

His voice was talking business, but his lingering gaze spoke of a different agenda. Annis realised a little too late that it had probably been unwise to challenge him on that level. Struggling for an air of cool composure she uncrossed her legs and smoothed her skirt down towards her knees. Only the faintly amused curl of his well-made mouth revealed that he was aware of her retreat.

"Unfortunately, in his eagerness to beat the opposition, he overlooked one small flaw." There was something distinctly shark-like about his smile. "A serious toxic waste problem, which would cost millions to clear up."

"I remember that." She frowned. "He sold the land to the local Council."

"For a fraction of what he'd paid for it. The same thing happened six months later, except this time the land was near Peterborough, and the problem was flooding. You really would have thought that experience would have taught him a lesson, but I'm afraid his competitive instincts got the better of him. He tried to recoup his losses by borrowing money for a series of speculative ventures, and some of them did indeed yield a profit – albeit a small one. More often than not he was over-bidding, and even the recovery in land prices wasn't enough to bridge the difference. He was having difficulty even meeting the interest payments on the loans."

Annis had listened to the story with a growing sense of foreboding. She had had no idea…

"In the end he was so heavily in debt that he was faced with two choices. Sell the company, with the few assets it had left, or face bankruptcy. I made him an offer. Statham Holdings belongs to me."

CHAPTER TWO

THEO'S words were clear enough, but it took a few moments for Annis to absorb the sense of what she was hearing. The company - everything her father had worked for his whole life, sacrificing virtually everything to it - gone in the space of a few years, all through a handful of unwise investments?

No wonder he had had a heart attack.

And she hadn't known a thing about it, she reflected with a stab of remorse. She *should* have known. But then her father had never confided in her, any more than he had in her mother - he had never believed a woman's brain could be capable of understanding anything to do with business.

"You seem to know a great deal about my father's affairs," she remarked, slanting Theo a searching glance.

"Oh, didn't I mention it?" There was something utterly predatory about him, like a panther waiting to pounce on his prey. "It was me he was bidding against for those parcels of land."

She frowned. "But why would you bid for land if you knew it had..." Realisation dawned, cold and hard, before she had even finished her sentence. "You did it deliberately. You knew about the problems, and you lured him into a bidding war. You *intended* to drive him to bankruptcy."

"It was his own greed that drove him to bankruptcy." His voice was ice-cold. "He thought he'd spotted a quick bargain, and he didn't want to spend out money to get a proper survey done. I simply... nudged him along a little." The last words were accompanied by a smile which lacked any trace of humour. "He wasn't aware who he was bidding against, of course. That might have alerted him. And he wasn't aware who was providing his loans. He was just happy to take the money."

"But why?" she protested, bewildered. "What did my father ever do to you?"

That hard mouth curved into an enigmatic smile. "I suggest you ask your Uncle Charles about that."

She frowned, puzzled. "I most certainly will..."

She drew in a long, deep breath, struggling to come to terms with what she had learned. If it was really true – if her father had lost everything and Theo Lander now owned Statham Holdings… Well, it was a shock, and there was no doubt that it was going to make things difficult financially, but she would find a way to manage.

And she certainly had no intention of giving him the satisfaction of seeing the impact his announcement had had on her.

"Well, there doesn't seem to be any point discussing this further." Gathering the scattered threads of her composure, she rose gracefully to her feet. "At least if you own the company, I won't have the bother of trying to sell it," she added on a defiant note of flippancy.

He was leaning back in his chair again, a glint of appreciative amusement in those dark, dangerous eyes. "Perhaps I didn't make myself quite plain, Miss Statham," he said softly. "I'm not just talking about the company. Your father had sold out all his other investments over the past few years, and had taken out a substantial mortgage, secured against Oakwood Lodge. I'm afraid your inheritance has been reduced to... well, not much more than the clothes you stand up in."

And the way his gaze was sliding over her appeared to suggest that he would like to divest her of those, as well.

As the full import of his words sank into her brain, her knees felt suddenly weak, and she was forced to sit down again. Nothing? Not even the house? No - that was impossible. Her father would never have…

But apparently he had. Theo Lander was no fool – he would know that she would check everything he had said.

A bubble of panic rose to her throat. What about the horses? There was nowhere else for them to go. None of them were ready for re-homing yet - well, perhaps Cleo, if somewhere could be found for her and her foal. But for the rest...

With a single concession to sympathy, Theo pushed her coffee cup towards her. She picked it up and held it, her fingers wrapped around it as if absorbing its warmth against the sudden chill circulating in her veins.

"But... what am I going to do?" she protested, stunned into bewilderment.

"What most other young women in need of an income do," he returned brutally. "Get a job."

"A job?" She stared at him blankly. How could she possibly work, with all the horses to take care of? Some of them needed schooling every day if they were ever going to have a chance of living a normal life again.

"Yes, a job." He enunciated the words with a mocking clarity, as if he was speaking to a child. "You know, work for your living, like the rest of us peasants. Unless you can find another way to pay off the mortgage, of course? It's already nearly six months in arrears. If you fail to clear the outstanding amount by the end of the month, I'm afraid I shall have to foreclose."

"*You* hold the mortgage?" She stared at him in shock. That really *was* the last straw.

"That's right." A cool smile flickered across that hard face. As handsome as the devil... "You know, I've always rather fancied the idea of living in Oakwood Lodge." He reminded her of a jungle cat surveying his prey. "It's a nice place. And it would certainly be one in the eye for the town, don't you think, to have the son of Tom Lander living there?"

With an effort of will, she rallied her forces. "You... can't just throw me out." She was almost sure of the legal point. "At the very least you'd need to get a court order."

"True," he conceded with a casually dismissive gesture of his hand. "That would create a slight delay - nothing more. I'm not in a particular hurry - I find that the anticipation of victory can be almost as sweet as the victory itself."

His arrogant attitude ignited her anger. "Don't be so sure of yourself!" Her eyes flashed in icy fury as she slammed down her coffee cup. "You might think you're very clever, but you're nothing but… pond life."

It was an insult she had frequently heard her father use, but she had never thought she would be moved to use it herself. She wasn't sure if her legs would support her as she swept to her feet, swinging her handbag over her shoulder.

Acid rage was burning inside her – wouldn't she just love to wipe the smile from that smug face?

Her eye fell on her half-empty coffee cup, and before her brain had time to frame any conscious thought she had picked it up and hurled it across the desk at him. Then without even looking to check whether she had scored a hit, she turned on her heel and stormed from the room, slamming the door behind her so loudly it must have registered on the Richter scale.

Pond life. Theo Lander stood at the large window of his office - formerly George Statham's office – watching as she walked across the car-park, that long swathe of honey-gold hair gleaming in the spring sunshine, that neat derrière swaying beguilingly in that skimpy little nonsense of a skirt.

She reached her car – just the kind of pricey little sports job he would have expected – and to his amusement was forced to wriggle her way into the front seat, displaying as long and shapely a pair of legs as he had ever seen.

He had been a little surprised by her reaction to the investigators' file. He had anticipated anger, dismissal. Instead she had also shown an unexpected ability to laugh at herself.

Not that it changed anything, not by one iota.

A small smile lifted the corners of his hard mouth. *Pond life.* She would pay for that one, the little vixen. And he would enjoy every moment of it.

It wasn't the first time a Statham had called him that. The last time had been nine years ago, when he had helped his father throw George Statham bodily out of their house. '*I won't let you stand in my way, Lander,*' he had hurled at them as he had stormed off down the path. '*You're pond life, the pair of you.*'

His father had just laughed, confident that Statham could do nothing to harm him. How wrong he had been.

Theo's hand balled into a fist as he stood gazing out of the window, and he struck it against the side of the wooden frame. This was just about the spot where their house had stood - that tree over there on the far side of the roundabout was the tree he used to climb when he was a kid.

They had only had a couple of acres, scrubby land mostly, not worth much as it stood. But it had been crucial to the development of the site, providing access to the main road. Without it, the surrounding land – Statham's land - would have been almost worthless.

If he had had any doubts about who had framed his father, Statham's arrogance had disabused him. He hadn't been able to resist coming to gloat, the day he had taken possession of the deeds.

He had driven up in his gleaming Rolls Royce, parking carefully in the muddy lane, and lowered the window to watch as the people who had bought the contents of the house had loaded up their van.

'*I warned you, Lander,*' he had sneered as Theo had stood by the gate, waiting to take the keys when the men had finished. '*You and your father. You shouldn't have tried to stand in my way.*'

It had taken nine long years to make him choke on those words. But it had been worth every grinding moment of hard work to see the look on his face when he had realised who was behind the company to which he was in so much debt. That one was for you, Dad.

But the daughter... That one's for me, he vowed with a grim smile.

Annis had to force herself to drive home slowly - in the frame of mind she was in, she could easily have broken the speed limit twice over. Damn Theo Lander - why had he come back to Ridgely anyway? She would have thought it would be the last place he would want to be after what had happened all those years ago.

But clearly he didn't feel any kind of shame about it - on the contrary, he appeared to be as bold as brass.

She was still on edge when she arrived home, and really not in the right frame of mind to have to deal with Uncle Charles. But his car was parked on the swooping gravel drive in front of the house. With a small sigh she let herself in through the front door.

The scent of bees-wax immediately tickled her nostrils - Joan, who came in three mornings a week to clean, was polishing in the dining room. She greeted her as cheerfully as she could manage, and went in search of the old man.

She found him in the sitting room at the back of the house, standing by the French windows that looked out over the terrace and the gardens, his hands clasped behind his back. The way he was rocking on his heels betrayed his agitation. He turned as she came into the room.

"Well?" he demanded harshly. "What did he have to say to you?"

Annis kept herself very composed as she walked across the room to take a seat in one of the armchairs. "Apparently he owns everything - the company, the house... Unless I can come up with enough money to keep up the repayments on the mortgage Dad took out, I shall be evicted."

Uncle Charles was actually her father's cousin, not her Uncle, but she had always given him the courtesy title. A prominent citizen of the town, he had considerable regard for his own importance - a solicitor and a local councillor, and the Chairman of the Planning Committee. He appeared to take the unexpected turn of events as a personal affront, as if he was the one whose entire future had suddenly been thrown into question.

"Well! I must say I never thought it would come to this," he fumed. "A dreadful state of affairs - dreadful. I had no idea your father was in such serious difficulties. If he had listened to my advice... But to have lost everything, in just a few years, after everything… I don't think I was ever more shocked in my life!"

Unfortunately not so shocked as to render him speechless, Annis mused dryly.

"I might have guessed young Lander would be trouble, as soon as he reappeared on the scene." He had taken to pacing from the window to the fireplace and back again. "You would have thought after what happened he would have had the decency never to show his face in this town again."

Annis slanted him a questioning glance. "What exactly *did* happen? Why did his father go to prison?"

Uncle Charles shrugged, dismissive. "Something to do with stolen cars. 'Ringing', they call it - much the same kind of thing as in the horse racing fraternity. They take a stolen car, and give it a new identity - change the number plates, file off the vehicle identification number - so they can pass it off as a legitimate vehicle. Quite a lucrative little business, I gather."

"But what did my father have to do with it?"

"Your father?" He appeared shocked by her question. "Why, nothing - absolutely nothing."

"Then why has Theo Lander picked on us like this?" She frowned, pursuing a line of thought which had been puzzling her ever since she had stormed out of the office which had once been her father's. "It must have cost him a great deal of money to have bought up the company, let alone take on the mortgage. Why would he do that? There has to be some kind of reason."

"It's just jealous spite." The old man's voice was laced with contempt. "Someone like that would hate to see anyone else better off. It's nothing more than petty vindictiveness."

Annis shook her head slowly. "No... No, it's more than that." Somehow, much as she hated him, she couldn't imagine Theo Lander doing anything petty. "There are plenty of people in Ridgely easily as well off as us. No - this is personal."

"Well, I'm sure I don't know what it is." To her surprise, Uncle Charles looked a little uncomfortable, his eyes evading her questioning stare. "Well, I suppose... It could be something to do with the fact that your father bought their house off them, after the trial. The house, and a couple of acres of land down by Lansdowne Lane."

"Where the business park is now?"

"That's right. It was pretty scrubby land, not much use for anything. Orchard, it was – can't have made much money out of that. And he gave them a fair price for it." Once again he was his usual forceful self. "Well, considering that they needed a quick sale. A very fair price."

"Which he very quickly turned into a substantial profit when he built the business park." It was a typical tactic of her father's - moving in swiftly to take advantage of someone else's misfortune. Perhaps it was little wonder that Theo Lander should have resented it - and had taken the opportunity to turn the tables when her father had found himself in difficulty.

So - at least she knew what she was up against now. Someone who was out for revenge, pure and simple, and had very few scruples about how he got it. But his quarrel had been with her father, she reflected with a frown. Why should he continue to take it out on her?

♥

"*Income twenty pounds, expenditure nineteen pounds nineteen shillings and sixpence - result happiness,*" Annis quoted, a twist of bitter humour in her voice. "*Income twenty pounds, expenditure twenty pounds ought and sixpence - result misery.* Thank you for those few words of wisdom, Mr.Micawber."

She was sitting in her father's old study, papers scattered all over the desk, chewing on the end of her pen. On a sheet of paper in front of her there were several columns of figures. Maybe if she used a pocket calculator...

But she knew only too well that no matter which way she tried to add them up, they would tell the same depressing story.

She had never really thought very much about how much she loved this house. It was simply her home, the place where she had grown up, where her roots delved deep into the soft, dark earth. It had belonged to her mother's family for generations - her great-grandfather had inherited it from *his* grandfather.

A pleasant mid-Victorian manor house, it had been built before the more grotesque excesses of the period had rendered the architecture ugly. Of hard grey Yorkshire granite, veiled with ivy, it stood in its own wooded grounds which sloped down to the river, just far enough from the by-pass for the traffic noise to be quietened to a background whisper.

When her mother had died it had passed, of course, to her father, but she had always assumed, as simply as night follows day, that eventually it would be hers. But now that solid ground had been swept from beneath her feet.

Her mouth thinned in anger. Although legally the house had not been left in trust, he should have seen it that way. He had no right to use it as security on a loan, no matter how desperate he was.

But he had - and now she was left with a huge debt that she didn't know how she could possibly repay.

But somehow she had to. She *couldn't* lose the house. And least of all to Theo Lander. If only she had a little more time… Unfortunately, at twenty five years old, she had no job and no qualifications. She had been planning to go to University when she had left school, but then her mother had become ill…

The only skill she had was with horses. Maybe she could open a riding stables, or even translate her ability to school troubled horses into some kind of income?

But it would take time to set that up, and time was what she didn't have. Tossing her pen down, she sat back in the big winged chair with a sigh, picking up the letter from Theo Lander's lawyer and re-reading it slowly. It still said exactly the same as it had said the last half-dozen times she had read it.

The warning was couched in formal legal jargon, but the threat was unmistakable. The mortgage on the house was six months in arrears - repayment was demanded immediately, or they would begin court proceedings for repossession.

The numbers, in bold print, seemed to dance in front of her eyes. Where on earth was she going to get that sort of money at short notice? She had a small trust fund from her mother, but that would just barely cover her living expenses, even pared to the bone.

She had already sold her father's two cars - unfortunately the Rolls Royce had been almost forty years old, a fact disguised by its personalised number-plate. She had actually got less for it than she had for the Volvo. And she could sell her own car, and just rely on the old Land-Rover she used to tow the horse-box.

But that wouldn't cover even half of the arrears. Maybe she could sell something else? she mused a little desperately. But what? A quick survey of the room suggested few possibilities.

There were shelf-loads of old books, but it wasn't very likely that they would fetch very much, unless she was lucky enough to find a rare first edition among them - and that sort of luck never cropped up when you needed it. There was a silver tankard - that must be worth a few pounds. And the clock on the mantelpiece might be an antique...?

Of course, there was her jewellery. She had stacks of it that she never even wore - most of it had belonged to her grandmother. Not that they were really family heirlooms, she assured herself quickly as a sharp twinge of guilt stabbed into her. Besides, they would do much more good helping to keep a roof over her head than sitting upstairs in her jewellery box.

The decision made, she bounced to her feet - if she was going to do it, she might as well do it right now. Skipping up the stairs to her bedroom, she pulled the marquetry box out of the cupboard, spilling the contents onto the bed to sort through it.

There were several rings, including one with quite a decent-sized ruby in it, an ugly old diamond brooch, a couple of old-fashioned necklaces and fussy pendants on gold chains, a heavy gold locket... No, on second thoughts she put that back - it had been her mother's favourite.

She piled all the rest into an old handbag, and then tackled her wardrobe. She had loads of dresses which she rarely wore – stuff she had bought on trips down to London, when she had gone to stay with her wild cousins.

There were several shops in York that bought designer wear in good condition to sell on second-hand. She might get something for them.

Putting it all together, it must add up to a reasonable amount. Maybe not enough to postpone the inevitable for very long, unless she could persuade Theo Lander to agree to reschedule the mortgage over a longer period so that she could pay off the interest. But at least she would feel as if she was doing *something*.

Half an hour later she had carefully folded half-a-dozen of her least worn and most expensive dresses into plastic bags, and carried them down to the car.

It had started to rain, one of those sudden spring showers, but she decided not to bother changing her light jacket for a raincoat - it would have stopped again in a little while, and anyway she had her umbrella if she needed it. She flicked on the windscreen wipers as she started the car and pulled out onto the lane.

As she swung around the roundabout onto the by-pass she felt the car slide a little - the road must be slippery from the rain. But there wasn't too much traffic - she could be in York by one o'clock. Once she had disposed of the dresses, she could have lunch in one of her favourite little coffee bars in the Shambles – that could be a luxury she wasn't going to be able to afford again for a while!

She took the next roundabout with care, putting her foot down as she hit the straight and accelerating smoothly to overtake a slow lorry, one finger tapping on the steering wheel in time to the rock music pouring from the CD player.

The next roundabout was coming up, and she deftly shifted down a gear, checking that nothing was approaching as she gave the wheel a slight turn… and suddenly the car slewed to the right.

Shocked, she managed to control the skid - fortunately there were no other cars too close. Damn - it wasn't the slippery road. She smacked her hand against the steering wheel, shaking her head. On top of everything else, she had a puncture. Now she was going to have to stop and change the wheel.

Oh well, there was nothing else for it - the first thing to do was to get off the roundabout and find a safe place on the busy dual-carriageway to stop.

Quickly reviewing the options, she drove on carefully around the roundabout and back towards Ridgely. There was a lay-by about fifty yards down, a bit muddy but safe from the passing traffic. At least it had stopped raining. She halted the car and clambered out, eyeing the flattened tyre with disgust. More expense, just when she didn't need it.

She opened the boot and shifted the bags onto the back seat, then lifted the floor panel to get out the jack and spare tyre - fortunately it was fully inflated. She was leaning across the driving seat to scrabble in the glove-box for the widget that unfastened the locking wheel-nuts when she heard a familiar cool voice behind her.

"Got a problem?"

Annis's heart kicked sharply against her ribs. Dammit, was he really the devil, appearing every time she suffered some kind of misfortune? Cautiously reversing out of the car, she straightened, uncomfortably aware of the interesting perspective he would have had of her neat rear end, pertly tipped in the air.

"No - I have a puncture. But I can manage, thank you."

"You're not afraid of breaking a nail?" Those dark eyes glinted with wicked amusement.

She disdained to answer, refusing to give him the satisfaction of knowing how much he disturbed her. Turning him an aloof shoulder, she gave her attention to the problem with the car.

She had never had to change a wheel before, but how difficult could it be? Obviously the first thing to do was to jack up the car, and she knew the important bit about making sure that she used the proper jacking points - once, when she had been in the sixth form at school, one of the lads had made the mistake of putting the jack in the wrong place, and had ended up punching a hole in his petrol tank. The rest of them had laughed about it for a week.

Coolly checking the diagram in the handbook, she found the right place, carefully making sure that the car was on reasonably level ground. Theo stood watching, leaning against the side of his own car, his arms folded across his wide chest, an expression of mild amusement on his face as if waiting for her to make a fool of herself. But she was doing everything right - the handbrake was on, the car wasn't in gear.

Pumping up the jack was hard work - he didn't offer to help, and she didn't ask for it. But flushed with success as she finally managed to lift the car enough for the wheel to be an inch off the ground, she couldn't resist slanting him a small smile of triumph. Next she had to work out how to get the wheel-nuts off. She frowned as she examined the widget - which way round did it go?

"Need a hand?" Theo enquired blandly.

She shook her head, calmly confident. "No thank you. As I said, I can manage."

Ah - she had to take the hub cover off first. Using the flat end of the wheel brace, she prised it up carefully until with a small click it dropped to the ground. Crouching on her haunches, she examined the nuts.

It was a bit fiddly getting the widget onto the nut and then slotting the wheel-brace into place, particularly when she was conscious of Theo watching her, just waiting for her to make a mess of it, but she managed it. Then drawing in a deep breath, she put her weight on the wheel-brace.

The only thing that happened was that the wheel spun round, and she lost her balance, scraping her hands and knees on the muddy ground.

"You should have loosened the nuts before jacking it up," Theo pointed out helpfully, his innocent expression not quite able to deny the laughter that was twitching the corners of his mouth. He was standing close behind her, watching over her shoulder, and she had to twist her head awkwardly to look up at him.

"So why the..." She swallowed the unladylike expression that was on the tip of her tongue. "Why didn't you tell me?"

He shrugged his wide shoulders in a gesture of lazy unconcern. "You said you didn't need any help."

She rose to her feet, brushing the dirt from her hands and knees. "All right, dammit - I do need some help." The words were dragged from her like pulling wisdom teeth.

He arched one dark eyebrow in mocking question, still

standing there with his arms folded, looking down at her - at five foot ten, and wearing heels, Annis was used to being able to look any man straight in the eye, and it was disconcerting to have to look up at him all the time.

"Please?" he prompted, deliberately provoking her.

Her jaw seemed to be locked in a vice, but she spat out the word. "Please."

He laughed, and she realised with a stab of annoyance that she had fallen into the trap of behaving exactly like the stuck-up bitch he seemed to think she was. But it was the only defence she had against him. The effect he had on her was much too powerful.

With a smile of lazy amusement, he stepped in and lowered the jack for her. She watched, fascinated, as with deft efficiency he fitted the wheel-brace onto the nuts one by one, treading it down with his foot to crank them loose. So that was how you did it!

Then he pumped the jack up again, those wide shoulders moving smoothly beneath the well-cut grey business suit he was wearing. The old wheel came off, and the new was one in place, the car back on the ground again and the nuts tightened in what couldn't have been much more than two minutes.

"There." He lifted the flat and put it back into the boot for her, along with the jack and the wheel-brace. As he closed the boot, he spotted the stuffed carrier bags on the back seat, many of them bearing the logos of top designer boutiques, and a glint of sardonic amusement flickered in those dark eyes, but he made no comment. "I'm sure you could have managed, but it seems a shame to get those pretty hands dirty."

"Thank you." Her voice sounded a little stiff to her own ears - being around him always seemed to do odd things to her heartbeat. "I'm… um… afraid you've got a bit muddy. There's a pub a little way down the road where you can clean up, if you want to."

"That's a good idea." His smile held a hint of challenge. "Perhaps you'll join me for a drink?"

Annis hesitated. A powerful instinct of self-preservation was warning her to get away from him as fast as she could. But then… if she was going to persuade him to give her more time to pay off the mortgage, she was going to have to swallow her pride and try to put their relationship on a slightly more friendly footing.

"Thank you." she conceded unsteadily, struggling to retain some semblance of dignity.

He nodded, his expression giving away nothing that would give her an excuse to back out. "Good. I'll see you there."

Not quite trusting herself to speak, she managed a weak smile and climbed back into her car.

CHAPTER THREE

ANNIS was sorely tempted to simply drive straight on past the pub, but the voice of wisdom prevailed. Much as she might hate to admit it, at the moment Theo Lander appeared to hold all the cards. And she would guess that he was not a man to cross.

She could manage one drink with him, surely? All she had to do was maintain a cool but friendly demeanour for half an hour or so – that couldn't be too difficult.

So she pulled her car into the car park and drew up alongside the sleek dark green Aston Martin just as he was climbing out from behind the wheel. The look of cynical amusement he slanted her way made her wonder if he had read her mind.

And the look of insolent approval as he let his gaze linger on her long legs as she swung from the car reminded her that the danger he represented was more than simply financial.

That thought made her pulse race with alarm. Dammit, what was wrong with her? It wasn't as if she wasn't used to being the object of male attention – in fact she usually quite enjoyed it.

She had had no shortage of casual boyfriends, both here and down in London, on the rare occasions when she had let herself be whisked off by her Aunt Vicky to join her cousins' sophisticated whirl of shopping and society parties.

But none of them had ever made her pulse race the way Theo Lander did. Oh, there had been nothing wrong with them - in fact, most of them had been very nice young men. Too nice, perhaps. Somehow their kisses had never managed to arouse more than a mild warmth.

But Theo Lander was different. She couldn't imagine being able to hold him at arm's length, as she had every other man she had known. There was something about him which suggested that when he kissed a woman, she would know she had been kissed – and no other man would ever quite measure up after that.

Struggling to push such treacherous thoughts from her

mind, she fixed some kind of smile in place. "Well, we're here."

Those dark eyes glinted with teasing humour. "So it would appear."

Cool and friendly, she reminded herself sternly. Searching for some distraction, she cast her eyes over the smooth, powerful lines of the Aston Martin. "That's a nice car you've got."

"The Aston? Yes, it is." The gleam of pride in his eyes told her she had hit on a subject close to his heart.

"I suppose you've got several cars?"

"No – just the Aston. I can't drive more than one car at a time, so there doesn't seem much point in having half-a-dozen more sitting in the garage."

They strolled across to the pub's entrance, and he held open the door for her with what she suspected was mocking politeness. He followed her inside, glancing around with genuine pleasure.

"I remember this place. I'm glad they haven't spoiled it."

Annis found herself in sympathy with that remark. The pub was cosy and old-fashioned, the sort of place designers of modern pubs tried to recreate but could never quite capture.

The wood panelling was dark with generations of polish and good honest elbow-grease, the seats were upholstered with dark green moquette fixed in place with slightly tarnished brass studs, and the sepia-tinted photographs on the walls, mostly of local scenes, must have been taken in the 'thirties, to judge from the style of the cars and the clothes that the people were wearing.

But her mind wasn't really on the décor. She was much too conscious of Theo Lander, very close behind her, almost touching – she could feel the warmth of his breath against her ear as he spoke. A hot little shiver ran down her spine. She felt as if she was caught up in some kind of force-field that he was generating…

It took a supreme effort of will to break the spell. "I'll… um… just go and wash the mud off my hands," she managed, her voice sounding brittle to her own ears. "I won't be a moment."

In the safety of the washroom, she stared at her own reflection in the starkly-lit mirror above the sink. It was almost like looking at a stranger. The features were hers, but the eyes seemed to glitter with a fevered brightness, her lips were softly parted – as if in anticipation of a kiss…

Dammit, dammit dammit, she scolded herself fiercely. This was crazy. She was only going to have a drink with him, for goodness' sake! One drink. And here she was, reacting like some adolescent school-girl with a crush. She had grown out of that a long time ago. Turning on the tap, she splashed her wrists with cold water to cool her heated blood.

Nine years ago… but the memory was still as vivid if it had been yesterday…

♥ ♥ ♥ ♥ ♥

It was a beautiful morning, the sky a clear blue, the pale sun sparkling on the silver dew that carpeted the grass. She had taken Fergal for an early ride out on the moors before getting ready for school. The young horse had been a little skittish at first, but he was beginning to learn to mind his manners, especially after a long canter over the heather-clad hills above the town.

Breathless from the exhilarating exercise, she turned reluctantly down to the gate which led out onto the road just a few hundred yards from home. As she reached it, she realised with some surprise that there was a car parked in the lay-by, with its bonnet open. And with an odd little thud of her heart, she recognised the man leaning over the engine. Theo Lander.

She hesitated, not sure what to do. She had already cut it fine - if she rode around to the next gate, she would be late for school. So leaning down, she opened the gate, and nudged Fergal through.

But the horse took a highly-bred dislike to the strange car. He started to prance around, showing off. As she struggled to steady him, a stray branch of a hawthorn beside the gate snared her scarf.

Fortunately Theo didn't seem to have even noticed her.

Wary of drawing his attention, she reached over to try to untangle the scarf. But Fergal was having none of it, jibbing backwards and forwards, keeping her just a few tantalizing inches from reaching the branch.

All too conscious that the minutes were ticking away and she was going to earn herself a detention, she gave up trying to get Fergal to co-operate, and slid to the ground, aiming to climb onto the gate. But the scarf was still just out of reach...

Suddenly Theo was behind her, reaching up easily over her head to unhook the scarf neatly from the thorns.

"There you are."

He had never spoken to her before. His voice was low and slightly husky, lilting with a lazy amusement as if he was mocking her. He was tall - it was unusual for her to have to tilt her head to look up at anyone. And he was standing so close, his body hard-muscled and male, trapping her in the corner between the fence and the gate.

So close that she was aware of a subtle male scent that was stirring up all kinds of turmoil in her adolescent hormones.

Numbly she took the scarf from his hand, her heart thumping so hard that it was difficult to breathe. His eyes were so dark... as she gazed up into them, she felt as if she could drown in them...

She knew all about his reputation. Some of the girls in her class had older sisters who had been favoured with a ride on the back of his big Triumph motorbike. No girl was safe with him, they said.

And now she was alone with him, on this quiet back road, several miles from town... What would she do if he touched her? What would she do if he tried to kiss her?

Afraid that he would recognise her agitation and think her silly and childish, she tilted up her chin, putting on her most haughty expression, her coldest voice. "Thank you."

"Silk." He fingered the soft blue fabric she was clutching in her tense hand, those dark eyes glinting with something wicked. "It must be expensive. You ought to take better care of it."

"I said thank you," she retorted with frosty dignity. "Now

please get out of my way so I can remount my horse."

One dark, level eyebrow arched in surprise, and he stepped back. "I do beg your pardon." There was a sharp edge of sarcasm in his voice. "Forgive me for delaying you."

He leaned back against the car, his arms folded, watching her, clearly waiting for her to make a fool of herself by being unable to get back up into the saddle. But Fergal was behaving beautifully now. She edged him up close to the gate and climbed up onto the bars, and with the reins in one hand swung her leg across the saddle.

Easing the horse forward, she spared Theo Lander a single high-bred glare down her nose before turning Fergal onto the road and riding away at a brisk trot.

♥ ♥ ♥ ♥ ♥

Oh lord, had she really been that rude? She must have left Theo with the impression that she was a horrible little snob who thought herself above even having the good manners to thank someone properly for doing her a favour. Her only consolation was that it had been the most fleeting encounter, and a long time ago. There was no way he would still remember it.

'Cool and friendly.' Like a mantra she kept repeating the words as she washed her hands and brushed the down her skirt. 'Cool and friendly.' Drawing in a deep, steadying breath, she opened the door.

Theo leaned an elbow on the bar and took a sip of his ginger and soda. Annis had been hiding in the Ladies for a long time. That was good, he mused with a twist of his hard mouth. She was edgy, off-balance – still trying to deny that charge of sexual attraction that sizzled between them.

But she was as aware of it as he was - he could sense it in every agitated glance, in every suppressed little quiver of her body. The next few weeks promised to be very entertaining – very entertaining indeed.

The door opened, and she walked out. For a moment she stood, hesitating, and he watched her unseen. Yes, she really had grown into a beauty. That gleaming bright honey-gold hair was caught up in some kind of twisted knot, but he could imagine it loose and tumbled across his pillow.

Her eyes were an incredible violet blue, fringed by long, silky lashes, her skin was a flawless creamy satin - and her mouth, touched with just the faintest gloss of pink, curled beguiling at the corners as if always ready to smile.

She spotted him, and moved uncertainly towards him. She walked with the easy grace of a dancer, the sway of her slender hips highlighted by the chain belt slung low around her waist, those long, long legs emphasised by the high-heeled straw mules on her elegant feet.

And though she was slender, she had curves in all the right places he reflected, letting his eyes linger appreciatively over the firm swell of her breasts. That silk shirt was just sheer enough to afford him a tantalising glimpse of the delicate lace tracery of white bra cups beneath.

One day, quite soon, he promised himself, he would afford himself the pleasure of unfastening the tiny pearl buttons all the way down the front of that shirt, brushing aside the silk, unclasping that frivolous scrap of lingerie…

"I'm sorry I was so long." A delicate hint of pink had risen to her cheeks, as if she had known exactly what he was thinking. It fascinated him – he couldn't even remember the last time he had seen a girl blush. "I… had a smudge on my skirt, and it was difficult to get it off."

"I was beginning to think you might have changed your mind about having a drink with me, and dodged out of the back door," he teased with a touch of dry humour.

She shook her head, returning him a cool little smile. "That would be extremely bad manners, Mr.Lander." Why on earth she hadn't she done just that?

"Theo," he insisted. "What would you like to drink?"

"Oh... just a mineral water." She reached into her handbag for her purse. "And I'm buying the drinks. To thank you for changing my tyre."

He conceded a sardonic smile. "As you wish."

Annis felt her heartbeat, which she had only just managed to get under control, start racing again. From the moment she had stepped out of the Ladies she had felt him watching her with every step, had felt as if he was undressing her with his eyes.

Summoning the scattered threads of her composure, she tilted up her chin at a haughty angle, returning the appraisal boldly, feigning a confidence she was far from feeling.

He was wearing the standard businessman's uniform - grey suit, white shirt. But the formality was somewhat undercut by the casual way he had discarded his tie – if indeed he had even bothered to wear one – leaving his collar loosely unfastened, affording her a tantalising glimpse of that smattering of rough, dark, male hair that curled at the base of his throat.

And there was something in the way he was standing which further subverted the image - one arm resting on the bar, the other pushing back the front of his jacket as his hand was thrust deep into the pocket of his trousers.

Without any appearance of conscious intent, he conveyed a brand of raw masculinity that was barely concealed beneath the urbane surface.

Suddenly she found herself remembering much too vividly the way he used to look in a faded and oil-stained T-shirt, the hard muscles in his wide shoulders moving smoothly beneath that sun-bronzed skin. And once, one very hot summer's day, he had pulled the T-shirt off, revealing a washboard-lean, ridged stomach above the thick leather belt of his low-slung jeans...

Her mouth felt dry, and unconsciously she lapped out her tongue to moisten her lips - a gesture which he didn't fail to notice.

Fortunately the bar-man arrived just at that moment with her drink, a welcome distraction. As she paid for the drinks, Annis slanted a swift, wary glance around the bar. She had forgotten, when she had suggested this place, that a lot of people she knew were likely to be in here at lunchtime. She could see no-one yet, but it was still a little early.

"Why don't we... um... go and sit down?" she suggested carefully as she tucked her wallet back into her handbag.

"If you like." He reached for the lunch menu, as if he had only just noticed it. "I remember they always used to do a decent meal in here. Will you join me?"

Annis hesitated, searching for a plausible excuse - but her brain refused to co-operate. Somehow, when he looked at her with those dark, dangerous eyes every shred of rational thought just evaporated. And anyway, she told herself weakly, what could possibly happen - in broad daylight, in a busy pub…?

So she inclined her head in assent, returning him a smile which she hoped conveyed a self-assurance she was far from feeling. "Yes, if you like." She had aimed for a lightness of tone, but she wasn't quite sure if she had hit it right. If she could convince herself that his presence had no effect on her whatsoever, perhaps she could convince him.

They ordered their meals, then carried their drinks through to the dining area. Theo glanced around, memories resurfacing. He'd come here quite often, back in the day. Was the old pool table still where it had always stood in the public bar?

He hadn't planned to stay on after the funeral - in fact, he really hadn't planned to attend the funeral in the first place. Some impulse – maybe to find closure? – had drawn him.

His lawyers could have dealt with settling up the affairs of Statham Holdings. He had fully intended to break it up, sell off the pieces, sell the house, and never set foot in the town again.

But then he had met the staff, all anxious about their jobs, all eager to show him what they could do.

He knew nothing about property development – but here were people who did. And after all, there were aspects of his own business that he knew little about – he hired experts, and listened to their advice. There was no reason why he couldn't do the same with Statham Holdings.

And then there was Annis.

She fascinated him, with her frosty dignity and her unexpected flashes of humour, and her total refusal to be intimidated by him. And he was pretty sure that she was as aware of that frisson of sexual tension between them as he was. But she was trying to fight it.

That was good – he had always enjoyed a challenge.

Annis would have preferred to hide away at a corner table, but Theo had steered her instead to one beside the window that looked out over the rain-soaked garden, now spangled with diamonds as the bright spring sunshine reappeared from behind the clouds, sparkling on the droplets of water clinging to the grass.

But she wasn't really seeing the view. She was much too conscious of the man sitting opposite her.

Perhaps it was only natural that she should find it difficult to deal with him, she tried to reassure herself, though not with much conviction. After all, she was in a particularly vulnerable state at the moment, with the shock of her father's sudden death, swiftly followed by the discovery of the financial mess he had left her in.

A mess which placed her almost totally in Theo Lander's power.

She could feel his dark eyes watching her across the table, could feel the faint prickle of her skin, as if he was touching her, caressing her...

Cool and friendly... "So, where have you been since you left Ridgely?" she enquired with polite interest, dropping her hands into her lap – pleating her napkin was *so* not a good look.

He smiled, those dark eyes taunting her. "You're going to pretend you didn't Google me?"

"I..." It was on the tip of her tongue to deny it, but she knew he wouldn't believe her. "Well of course I did. What did you expect? It wasn't particularly difficult – you're on the Forbes 500. But not very high," she couldn't resist adding.

"High enough." Those dark eyes glinted with amusement. "And every penny legally earned."

"Yes… I saw. I couldn't understand much of it, though," she admitted wryly. "Something to do with an engine component that reduces fuel consumption?"

He nodded. "At very high speeds. I had a buddy who was a mechanic with a Formula One racing team, so when I decided to bail out of Ridgely I got in touch with him and he lined me up with a job. I worked for them for a couple of years – that gave me the opportunity to develop my original ideas. It's fitted now in virtually all racing cars, and most high-performance road cars all over the world. We're also adapting it for use in aero-engines, and the military are interested in a further modification for their tanks and APCs."

"You've done pretty well for yourself out of one little gizmo." In spite of her determination to maintain a nonchalant front she was genuinely impressed.

"It's quite a useful little gizmo. And there have been a few more gizmos since then. Now we've developed a new hybrid engine, with a higher power ratio – it's being track-tested down at Donnington Park at the moment, and it should be going into full production next year."

"Uncle Charles called you a second hand car salesman."

That made him laugh. "Well, I am a partner in a car dealership. But it's not quite the sort of back-lot scrap-yard your uncle was probably trying to imply. You wouldn't get much change out of 100K for the cars we sell."

"And yet you still take the time to persecute a man over some stupid grudge from nine years ago," she challenged, her eyes flashing ice.

His mouth hardened. "As I suggested the other day, you need to ask your Uncle Charles about that 'stupid grudge'. I suspect he knows a great deal more about it that he's told you."

Annis frowned. She had suspected that herself, after her last conversation with her uncle. But it was pretty clear that he wasn't going to talk about it – when she had tried to ask him more questions he had just got angry, insisting that there was nothing more to tell.

Theo was leaning back in his seat, watching her across

the table, that wicked glint back in his eyes. "Mind you, I have to admire your spirit. Even with bankruptcy staring you in the face, you just couldn't resist going out and buying yourself a new dress. In fact several new dresses, by the look of it."

She was about to tell him that she was taking them to sell, but a sharp stab of pride changed her mind. Instead she shrugged her slim shoulders in a dismissive gesture. "I need something decent to wear. You wouldn't expect me to walk around in rags, would you?"

He conceded an appreciative laugh, letting his gaze flicker briefly down over her slim curves in a way that made her breath feel hot in her throat. "I'm sure you'd look sensational in a potato sack."

"Anyway, I'm not bankrupt." *Cool and friendly…* Damn him - he was making it very difficult. "I'll pay you back every penny."

"I'm glad to hear it." Mocking amusement lifted the corners of that intriguingly sensual mouth. "Mind you, you don't have long. I'm sure you've had the letter from my lawyer by now?"

Her eyes answered him, flashing with cold fury.

"So what's the plan?" He was deliberately trying to goad her into losing her temper. "You seemed to feel that getting a job was quite beneath you. So what else is there? Snaring a rich husband, perhaps? Some chinless wonder with clammy hands and jug ears, and a nice juicy trust fund to play with? Or maybe you're desperate enough to settle for old and fat."

"Whatever I decide to do, it's my business." she retorted, retreating behind a facade of frosty disdain.

He shook his head, mock-serious. "Don't you know what they say? If you marry for money, you end up paying for it - on your back. Don't do it - it would be a terrible waste. You don't want a man with clammy hands in your bed. You need a real man - one who'll know just how to touch you, how to melt through that icy shell and set your body on fire."

His voice had taken on a huskier timbre, and Annis could feel her skin growing hot, just as if those strong, sensitive hands really were caressing her. "Like you, I suppose?" she choked out.

He smiled slowly, as if considering the suggestion. "Possibly. Except that I wouldn't marry you. Oh, I might be prepared to keep you in the frocks and fripperies you're so fond of. But I wouldn't marry you."

Annis felt a surge of anger boiling up inside her. "Don't fool yourself that's ever going to happen," she hissed fiercely, slamming her napkin down on the table and surging to her feet. "You're the last man on this earth I'd ever go to bed with…"

"Two mushroom and tomato?" The waitress, arriving untimely with their soup, stepped back quickly to avoid a messy collision.

At the same moment Annis spotted some people she knew in the bar. She sat down abruptly. Worse than being seen having lunch with Theo Lander would be being seen storming out on him. "Oh… Um… I'm sorry…" she mumbled with an apologetic smile to the waitress, conscious of the hot pink that had rushed to her cheeks.

The waitress, looking faintly relieved, set the bowls down in front of them and retrieved a basket of bread rolls from the side-board. By the time she had gone, Annis had managed to regain some semblance of composure.

Across the table, those dark eyes glinted with wicked amusement, but he said nothing - apparently he had decided that he had goaded her far enough for the time being. Instead, as he sipped his soup, he turned the conversation onto neutral lines.

"There seem to have been a lot of changes in the town since I've been away," he remarked blandly. "I noticed that quite a few of the shops along the High Street are empty."

She had to take a discreet sip of her mineral water to moisten her dry mouth. "Y… Yes. Her heart was still beating uncomfortably fast, but her voice was commendably even. "They opened a new retail park at the top of Emstrey Road about five years ago – it's taken a lot of the trade."

"Pity." He shook his head. "It makes the place look dead with so many boarded-up shop-fronts."

Annis privately agreed with him. What she didn't mention was that it was Uncle Charles, in his office as Chairman of the Planning Committee, who had approved the scheme. And her father who had built it.

"At least the traffic has eased a lot since they built the by-pass," Theo went on easily. "I remember when the place was so choked with heavy lorries you took your life in your hands just crossing the road, even at the traffic lights."

She nodded. "Yes, it's made it a lot better - especially for the older people and the mothers taking their children to school. You can even ride down it now - though not in the rush-hour, of course. It still gets quite busy then. And it's made it much easier for the through traffic, wanting to get to York – it's cut the journey time right down. Sometimes it used to take you twenty minutes just to get from the King's Oak to the bridge."

She was aware that she was babbling to cover her tension, but for all her good intentions it was very difficult to retain her equilibrium when he was sitting there watching her with those dark, level eyes. It was impossible to read what he was thinking – but she was inclined to think it would be better if she didn't know.

She reached out a slightly unsteady hand for her glass, and took another sip of her mineral water. Maybe she should have ordered wine... But no, perhaps it was better that she hadn't, she reflected edgily - she couldn't risk letting alcohol fuddle her brain.

The pub was famous for its traditional English food. The soup was replaced by a fillet of lamb so tender that it seemed to melt in her mouth, served with a piquant red-current sauce and delicately cooked vegetables, and the sweet freshness of the local bottled spa water was a perfect complement to the meal.

And the conversation was easy, too - though afterwards Annis couldn't remember a thing they'd talked about. She was surprised to find that Theo was an entertaining companion, with a finely-honed sense of humour that was similar to her own. Insensibly she found herself beginning to relax a little, to actually enjoy herself...

But it would be dangerous to let herself relax too much, she warned herself warily. It would be far too easy to let herself fall under the spell of that smooth charm. She couldn't afford to let herself forget what lay behind it. He was threatening to evict her from her home, force her to close her stables, just to gain some kind of twisted revenge on her father.

The waitress came to take their plates, and they both passed on desert in favour of coffee. Annis stirred a swirl of cream into hers, listening absently as Theo reminisced about a time when the river had flooded all along the High Street, and he had thought it was great fun to walk to school along the duck-boards which had been hastily erected by the Town Council. She couldn't help but smile, picturing him as that dark-haired little boy, splashing along in his Wellington boots.

Maybe if she told him about the horses, appealed to his better nature...

But so far she hadn't seen any evidence that he *had* a better nature, she reminded herself wryly. What she knew of him suggested that he was totally without scruples. And the last thing she wanted was to give him an additional weapon to use against her...

A sudden burst of laughter from the main bar caught her attention; loud voices, a head of blonde highlights half turned away. Dammit, that was all she needed! Lucinda Forsyth. It you wanted the whole world to know your business, just tell Lucy. Discreetly she edged her chair back a little, so that she was better concealed by the screen which separated the dining room from the rest of the pub.

But Theo had noticed her movement, and arched one quizzical eyebrow "What's wrong?" he enquired, a sardonic inflection in his voice. "You keep watching the bar, as if you're ready to drop your napkin and dive under the table after it in case any of your friends should happen to see you having lunch with me."

"What? Of... Of course not. I" But she knew that the hot blush that had risen to her cheeks betrayed her in the lie.

"Oh, don't bother denying it - you've been like a cat on a hot tin roof ever since we came in here. As if you're ashamed to be seen with me - Miss Annis Statham, the town's high-nosed Princess, consorting with the reprobate Theo Lander? Whatever would people say?" His eyes glinted darkly. "I wonder how many of your so-called friends will still want to know you when they find out you're broke? Will any of them help you when you find yourself out on the street?"

His voice was hard with contempt, and she felt the sting of tears in her eyes. But she fought them back - she wasn't going to give him the chance to accuse her of playing for his sympathy. "I can pay the mortgage. If you'd just give me a little more time."

He arched one dark eyebrow in quizzical amusement. "You seem to have a rather optimistic view of my generosity. Why should I wait any longer for my money, when your father has already kept me waiting for nearly six months?"

Annis couldn't find a reply - there was really nothing to say.

"However..." He paused, as if considering his words. "I might be prepared to offer you a... proposition."

"A proposition?" She glanced across at him in sharp suspicion. "What kind of proposition?"

"I was originally planning to break up and sell off the whole of the Statham property portfolio. But I've changed my mind. I've decided to transfer all my operations here instead."

"Here? You mean... to Ridgely?" She stared at him across the table in startled amazement. "Why?"

He shrugged those wide shoulders. "It's my home town - even if I'm considered *persona non grata* by some."

That was a point there was no arguing with. "So why would you want to stay?"

"Because it's my home town. And I hate to see it looking so run-down. The place needs new houses, new shops – and most of all, jobs. I'll move my research and development team up here first, then the manufacturing arm next year. It's a very convenient location – not too far from the motorway, and the house prices are good. I'll be able to offer high-quality engineering apprenticeships, opportunities for advanced computer-based design skills."

She continued to stare at him. She certainly hadn't expected something like that. "That… should give the local economy quite a boost," she conceded.

"Of course, your father's office is going to need quite a bit of refurbishment. I really don't think I could stand all that fake Victorian splendour around me."

"Oh…" That all sounded pretty permanent.

"The point is…" He paused as the waitress returned to take their plates and offer coffee. "If I'm going to do that without too much obstruction, I need to get the town on my side."

"You shouldn't have much trouble, if you're going to invest good money," she pointed out cynically. "Although the likes of Uncle Charles wouldn't like it.

He smiled, that cool, arrogant smile. "Oh, money can go a long way - there'll be plenty of people who once wouldn't have given me the time of day who now would fall over themselves to smile and shake my hand. But I know this town. Behind the smiles, the old attitudes are still ingrained - the snobbery, the prejudice. I'm still the town's bad boy, the son of a man who went to prison."

"If that's the way you choose to look at it."

"That's the way it is." He laughed without humour, lounging back in his seat again. "Oh, it doesn't bother me personally what they think of me - I don't give that for their small-minded opinions." He snapped his fingers in a gesture of contempt. "But business is another matter. I don't want to find doors closed against me simply because of the town's hostility. Which is where you come in."

"Me?"

He nodded. "I need to borrow a little of your social cachet, to smooth my path towards respectability. If people see us together as friends… or even more than friends…"

Her eyes blazed cold contempt. "And why would I even *think* of doing that?"

"Well, if the benefits to the town aren't enough to

convince you, maybe you should remember that I hold the mortgage on your house - and I'm about to foreclose." If she had let herself forget for a fraction of a second just how ruthless he could be, the hard note in his voice was a timely reminder. "But if you agree to my… proposition, I would be willing to delay taking any action. And for the duration, I would waive any interest payments. Shall we say… until Christmas? That would give me sufficient time to establish myself, and it would give you time to get your financial situation in order – at the very least, to find somewhere else to live."

"That's… blackmail!"

He regarded her with amusement, those dark eyes glinting dangerously. "Not at all. Our interests merely coincide."

"And everyone will think that I'm… that I'm your mistress."

"What a delightfully old-fashioned word for it. But yes, I suppose they will." His manner was as coolly matter-of-fact as if he had just offered her a job in the typing pool. "Of course, it would mean that during that time you would not be able to date anyone else – that would rather undermine the credibility of the exercise. I assume that won't be a problem?"

Her anger and outrage found expression in a brittle laugh. "It won't be a problem because I'm not going to do it." Her voice was laced with icy scorn. "And besides, no-one would believe for one moment that I was dating you. Not in a million years!"

She stared across the table at him, a little breathless, and more than a little nervous – rather belatedly she had realised that it might not be a good idea to antagonise him. But he merely laughed in lazy mockery - though she couldn't miss the glint of steel in those dark, level eyes.

"You know, I like it when you play the haughty ice-princess. It amuses me. You wouldn't be so haughty if you really *were* my mistress." He smiled slowly, letting his gaze drift down over her body as if he was stripping off her clothes, one by one. "Lying there across my bed, naked, that golden hair spread out across the pillows... No, I don't think you'd be so haughty then."

Annis felt herself grow hot at the image he had conjured so explicitly, and was forced to draw in a long, deep breath as she struggled to maintain some semblance of composure. "You might be able to hold that mortgage over me as some kind of threat," she hissed, "but there's no way I'm ever going to be your mistress - pretend or otherwise."

She was burning her boats, but there was nothing else she could do. He had goaded her beyond all endurance. She wasn't sure if her legs would support her as she swept to her feet, swinging her handbag over her shoulder.

"I'm afraid we have nothing more to say to each other." Her eyes flashed like ice on fire as she rose to her feet. "Good afternoon, Mr.Lander."

CHAPTER FOUR

IT WAS a beautiful morning. High on the rolling hills above the town, a fresh breeze was blowing, but the sun was warm. Annis sat relaxed in the saddle, gazing out over the wide green landscape before her, tears pricking at her eyes.

There wouldn't be many more mornings like this, when she and Fergal could canter out over the soft, springy turf, with only the sheep for company.

She stroked her hand down over the quivering curve of the horse's neck, then leaned down to wrap her arms around him, burying her face in the rough hair of his mane. It was three days since she had turned down Theo Lander's outrageous offer, and she had finally been forced to concede that her options had run out. Last night she had sat down and written out the advert: '***15.1 hh Full Reg Connemara Gelding 11yrs old...***'

"I promise I'll find a good home for you," she whispered, her voice breaking. "Somewhere they'll love you – though not nearly as much as I do."

With a small sigh she sat up, and with a nudge of her heels urged the horse into a long, loping gallop along the grassy slope. She must try not to think about the future – it was just too painful.

Whatever else she might say about her father, he had never minded how much money it had cost to run the stables. The Rescue Society helped out as much as they could, of course, but with the cost of feed and good bedding, not to mention veterinary fees – though Vicky charged only costs - it was an expensive enterprise.

If she'd known about her father's financial problems... But he had chosen not to tell her. He'd gone on paying her allowance, the same as always – he'd even bought her that flashy new red sports car for her birthday, though she'd been quite happy with her little mini. Not, she suspected, because he had been trying to shelter her from an unpleasant reality, but because it was part of his nature to always put on a front.

So she wasn't going to take the blame. It was Theo

Lander who was responsible for this mess – Theo Lander, with his hard eyes and his ruthless desire for revenge. Because of him, she had lost everything she cared about in her life.

Letting herself through the gate from the lower field and closing it behind her, she turned carefully onto the road, trotting along for a hundred yards or so before turning into the narrow lane which led up to the house. The trees were in full summer leaf, hiding the house until she was quite close…

Fergal skipped abruptly sideways, reacting to her unexpected tug on the reins. Dammit – think of the Devil, and he appears… Parked on the gravel sweep of the drive was a sleek dark green Aston Martin.

She brought the horse skilfully under control and rode up to the car as Theo opened the door and climbed out. He was casually dressed today, in well-cut denim jeans and a dark blue cashmere sweater – but though the look was casual, she didn't need to see any labels to know that it was all of the finest quality.

And that soft cashmere was moulded across shoulders as impressively broad, a stomach as lean and hard as nine years ago.

"Good morning." His greeting was impeccably polite, though the smile that lifted the corners of his hard mouth was lazily mocking.

Fergal jibbed again, and for a moment Annis had to focus on steadying him. "What are you doing here?"

"I thought I'd come over and have a look at my new house. Perhaps think about what sort of changes I might want to make when I move in. It looks like it could do with a fair bit of modernisation." He glanced up at the ivy-draped façade. "Has it got central heating?"

His insolence made her blood boil "It isn't yours yet," she snapped.

"Not *yet*." The glint of cynical amusement in his dark eyes suggested that he was deliberately provoking her. "By the way, did I mention the penalty clauses in the mortgage? Arrears accrue at an additional two percent."

"I saw that," she spat. "I have read the documents."

"Very wise of you." His eyes moved from her to Fergal, registering appreciation. "Nice horse."

"Yes." She didn't want him to come near Fergal, didn't want him to have anything to do with him. It was because of him that she was having to sell her beloved horse.

"I've heard keeping horses is a pretty expensive hobby. But I suppose Daddy never minded paying out for anything his little girl wanted, did he? How are you going to manage now?"

"I'll manage." *Somehow*, she added under her breath. It wasn't just Fergal she had to worry about – it would be fairly easy to find a good home for him. But the others…

Poor Silver still shied at loud noises, and Patches would always limp slightly from the nasty injury to his fetlock from having been tethered by a rope. Then there were Dolly and Polly, too old to be uprooted even if a home could be found for them.

"The mortgage payments are more than six months in arrears," he reminded her ruthlessly. "And with nothing but your trust fund to live on…"

She didn't answer – she couldn't answer. Tears had risen to choke her throat, but she wasn't going to let him see her cry. Sliding down from the saddle, she moved round to fiddle with Fergal's bridle, keeping her back to Theo.

"How are you going to keep him *and* pay the mortgage?" His voice was softer, but still persistent. "Even if you were qualified for anything, there aren't many high-paying jobs around here."

"I know that." She couldn't stop her voice from cracking. She dropped Fergal's bridle and wrapped her arms around his neck, burying her face against the warm muscle, breathing in the familiar scent of him – the smell of leather, of hay, of sunshine on a grassy meadow. The tears were soaking her cheeks now – she couldn't hold them back.

"There is an alternative."

"You've already told me your terms," she reminded him bitterly.

"A few months of accompanying me to public functions, dinner parties, that sort of thing – would that be so awful?

What's more important to you – your reputation, or your horse?" He paused for a moment to let that sink in. "I'll even improve my offer. At the end of the six months, I'll write off all the outstanding arrears. And I'll let you renegotiate the mortgage over a longer period, so that it would easier for you to pay."

She turned her head to stare at him. He had baited his hook with an offer he knew she would find almost impossible to resist. The chance of keeping the house, keeping the stables… Was her pride really worth more than that? "You'd reschedule the mortgage?"

He nodded.

"And it will be purely a business arrangement?" she queried unsteadily, her eyes narrowed in suspicion. "You won't expect me to…"

"Sleep with me?" His smile was coldly cynical. "I've never found it necessary to resort to financial coercion to get a woman into my bed. But of course if you should choose to…" His voice took on a husky tone, treacherously beguiling.

"I won't." She tilted up her chin, struggling to portray the image of the ice-princess he had accused her of being. "Very well. In public, I'll pose as your… girlfriend. But the act stops at the bedroom door."

"Agreed." He inclined his head in assent, but she couldn't miss the dangerous gleam in his dark eyes. He still intended to get her into his bed if he could.

♥ ♥ ♥

Annis stood in front of the long mirror in her dressing room, regarding her reflection with a critical eye. She had spent most of the day at the Country Club, helping to transform it for the Mid-Summer Ball, and then an hour down at the stables spreading hay for the horses who stayed out in the large paddock, and making sure that the rest were fed and watered and settled for the night. It had left her little time to get ready for the evening.

The Ball was one of the biggest annual events on the local social calendar, raising a shed-load of money for the children's hospice. And it was going to be her first public appearance at Theo's side.

She hadn't seen him for two weeks, and she had almost begun to let herself imagine that the whole thing had been some kind of bad dream. But three days ago she had received a telephone call.

"It's that annual shindig at the Country Club on Saturday night, isn't it?" He hadn't even bothered to say who was speaking – not that she could have been in the slightest doubt. "Get me a ticket."

Just like that! Anger surging to the surface, she had responded coolly, "I doubt that there'll be any left at such short notice."

"Oh, I think you'll find you can manage it," he had asserted, the hint of threat in his voice only thinly veiled. "Put me down as your Plus One. After all, you're on the committee, aren't you?"

Now how had he known that? Of course – Maggie had probably told him, in all innocence. Gritting her teeth, she had conceded the point. "Very well, I'll see what I can do."

"Good. I'm in Hong Kong, but I'll be back on Saturday morning. I'll pick you up at seven."

"Actually I already have a date…"

"Well *actually* you're going to have to tell him that you had forgotten you had a prior arrangement."

"I can't do that…"

"Yes you can. Seven o'clock."

He had cut the call before she could protest. "Damn the man." She had scowled at her own reflection in the big gilt-framed mirror above the fireplace in the sitting room. "As if he just has to snap his fingers, and I'm supposed to jump."

But that was the way it was, she mused bitterly. What had she ever done to him, that he was so intent on punishing her? Not content with stealing her inheritance and her home, he seemed intent on stealing her self-respect as well. He wanted to flaunt her like some kind of trophy in front of the scandalized eyes of the whole town.

Well, they may all believe she was his mistress, but she

would never let it be anything more than a pretence, she vowed grimly. That was one thing she would not surrender. Her bedroom door would remain firmly shut.

A small smile curved her soft mouth as she crossed the room to pick up her evening bag. The silk taffeta of the full-skirted ball-gown rustled as she walked. The dress wasn't the one she'd originally planned to wear this evening - that elegant little black sheath was still hanging in the wardrobe.

This one was of a rich teal blue, its strapless bodice cut low across the curve of her breasts. It might be a little over-the-top, but it was a far better bet if you didn't want anyone to get too close. The bones in the bodice were likely to stab them in the hand, and the layers of rustling petticoats enforced an exclusion zone a yard wide all round her.

She had underplayed the flamboyant style by putting her hair up into a modern spiky knot on the top of her head, and she wore no jewellery - chiefly because she had none left to wear after her depredations on her grandmother's collection. With luck, everyone would assume that she was setting a trend, letting her own clear, creamy skin be her only adornment.

A swift glance at her watch told her that it was just past five minutes to seven. She would guess that Theo would be precisely on time - and that he would be expecting her to keep him waiting. For that reason alone, she had no intention of doing so.

She swirled her cashmere wrap around her shoulders and snapped off the light. She had just reached the bottom of the stairs when she heard the crunch of car-tyres on the gravel of the drive.

With a quick step she moved across to stand behind the door, carefully easing the catch. The wood was quite thick, but she could hear the slam of the car door, followed by the sound of footsteps across the gravel, and then the absence of sound as he climbed the steps - one, two...

With flawless timing, she opened the door just as his hand reached up for the bell.

She had the satisfaction of catching him by surprise, but

he recovered almost instantly. The look in his dark eyes changed to one of open appreciation as they swept down over her, taking in the creamy curve of her bare shoulders, the soft swell of her breasts confined within the tight-ribbed constraint of the silk bodice. The high heels of her strappy evening sandals took her to a stately six feet tall, and the lights of the hall behind her glinted like burnished gold in her hair.

"Magnificent," he approved.

He was looking pretty magnificent himself, she was forced to concede, in a formal black dinner-jacket with a finely-pleated white shirt and a black silk bow-tie. But the elegance of the cut did nothing to disguise the uncompromising maleness of that tall, hard-muscled body, and with those level dark eyes and that hard, sensual mouth he was as handsome as the devil.

She drew in a long, deep breath of air, suddenly rather too aware of the way it lifted her breasts against the hard-boned bodice of her dress. But she had practised her opening line, and delivered it with just the right touch of cool humour.

"I'm afraid it's the butler's night off," she announced coolly as she stepped out into the night air, closing the front door behind her.

His lips twitched in appreciative response. "I wasn't expecting a butler, but I did expect to be kept cooling my heels until you deigned to be ready."

"Did you?" The delicate arch of one eyebrow concealed her pleasure at having second-guessed him so accurately. "I was always taught that punctuality is the politeness of kings."

"Is it indeed?" There was a lilt of teasing amusement in his voice. "And of ice-princesses, too, apparently."

She quickly suppressed an answering smile, her fine violet-blue eyes flashing him a look of frosty disdain as she picked up her skirt and trod carefully down the steps. He moved smoothly ahead of her and opened the car door, impeccably polite. "I hope your dress won't get crushed."

"I don't think it will be a problem." She settled into the deep comfort of the passenger seat, deftly twitching the folds of taffeta into place and bestowing them out of way as he closed the door and came round to climb in behind the steering wheel.

"I suppose you're more accustomed to driving around in Daddy's Rolls Royce?" he taunted.

She knew that he was trying to needle her, but she wasn't going to let him get under her skin. "Oh, I sold the Roller." She waved her hand in a dismissive gesture. She wasn't going to tell him how little she had got for it. "It was quite a nice car, but you couldn't really say they're fun to drive."

"True."

"Now this one is." Her languid pose was forgotten for a moment as she admired the discreetly luxurious interior of the Aston Martin. "This is what I *call* a car. A real thoroughbred."

And just the sort of car she would have expected him to drive, she reflected - as elegant as a gentleman's club, with all that pale cream Connolly hide on the seats and lining the doors. But unmistakably powerful - even asleep, the finely-tuned V12 engine beneath that long, curving bonnet seemed to radiate a latent warning. It was truly a driver's car.

He slanted her a smile of lazy amusement as he gunned the ignition. The engine purred into life like a big, sleek jungle-cat, awakened and ready to hunt. The wide tyres crunched quietly over the gravel as he turned in the circle of the driveway and out onto the lane, expertly holding all that power in check as the car seemed to want to spring forward like a panther on a leash.

He was watching the road ahead, which gave her the chance to study him covertly from beneath her lashes. That profile could almost have been carved from marble, she reflected fancifully - any sculptor would have been proud of those strong, clean lines, the nose that tended just slightly towards the aquiline, the firm, arrogant jaw.

And he was as hard as marble, she reminded herself, a small shiver feathering down her spine - cold and calculating, ruthlessly manipulating to get what he wanted. Like his take-over of her father's business.

She had been thinking about it a lot over the past couple

of weeks, and she was becoming convinced that there was more to it than mere vindictive spite, because her father had profited so handsomely from the purchase of his father's land.

Theo was a very successful businessman himself, after all - he must have pulled off more than a few tough deals in his time. But what could her father have done to trigger such a dark desire for revenge?

The traffic lights at the top of the High Street had turned red, and as Theo braked to a halt he glanced down at her, catching her watching him before she could turn her eyes away. "You seem deep in thought?"

Instantly defensive, Annis pinned a taut smile in place. "I was just wondering what people are going to say tonight."

"Nothing. When they see you in that dress, they'll all be speechless."

That forced a reluctant laugh from her, and he smiled in satisfaction as the lights changed again and he slid the car into gear.

"That's better. I was afraid you were going to give me the ice-princess treatment all evening, as punishment for making you break your date with... who was it you were supposed to be coming with?"

"Jeremy Cummings," she admitted with some reluctance.

"Jerry Cummings? That drip?" He laughed - a rich, slightly husky laugh that did odd things to her taut-strung nerve fibres. "Oh, I've definitely done you a favour then. I'm afraid you'd have been in for a deadly boring evening with old Jerry."

"I like him." She certainly wasn't going to admit that he was probably right.

"You'd walk all over him." His dark eyes glittered with wicked amusement. "And I bet he kisses like a wet fish."

The description was so cruelly accurate that she was forced to suppress the bubble of laughter that sprang to her lips. "He... He's a very nice person."

"I'm quite sure he is," Theo conceded on a note of dry humour. "But even though the stuck-up little bitch in you would prefer to be seen out with him, you'd far rather be kissed by me. Wouldn't you?"

His words brought a flame of scarlet to her cheeks. To be kissed by him...

And did he really think her a stuck-up bitch? That stung. Although she really shouldn't be surprised, she reflected with a wry honesty. She didn't know how to deal with him, and so she always put up that mask of frosty dignity to hide behind.

Unfortunately as a defence strategy it seemed to have backfired - he had taken it as a challenge, intent on knocking her down from her haughty perch. The trouble was, she didn't know what to do about it. She was very much afraid that if she were to lower her defences, even by a fraction, he would sweep right over them.

The Country Club was beside the river, just out past the fringes of the town. There were already quite a few cars in the car-park as Theo pulled into a vacant parking-slot and swung himself out from behind the wheel, walking around the front of the car to open her door for her.

He offered her his hand, the gallantry of the gesture undercut by the glint of sardonic amusement in those dark eyes.

"Thank you." Her voice was stiff and she withdrew her hand as soon as she was on her feet, shaking out the rustling taffeta of her skirts all around her.

That odd little tingle of heat that had seemed to be spreading from his touch must be purely her imagination, she chided herself as she swirled the luxurious Pashmina around her shoulders and picked up her skirts to move gracefully up the steps to the Club's entrance.

If she had hoped to slip in unnoticed, or have a moment to collect herself, she was disappointed. The elegant entrance hall was being patrolled by Rosemary Trenchard, the formidable chair of the Friends of the Hospice committee. Looking like some medieval dragoness in a sheath of leaf-green watered silk that moved like a suit of armour, she bore down on Annis the moment she stepped through the door.

"Annis, darling, thank goodness you're here. That dreadful man in the kitchen is being *so* difficult. I want them to start serving dinner at eight, but he won't even listen to me."

Annis smiled. It was the same every year – the Clash of the Titans. Monsieur László ran a top restaurant in York but gave up a busy Saturday night every year to support the charity. In the other corner was Rosemary who – though it was now five years since her husband had worn the Mayoral chain – was still known as the Lady Mayoress, so perfectly did the title seem to fit her.

"Don't worry," she soothed. "I'll go and speak to him. Um… by the way, I don't know if you've met… this is… Theo Lander."

Rosemary's polite society smile froze on her lips. "Theo…?"

"Lander," Theo supplied, taking the outstretched hand she had forgotten to withdraw. "I don't expect you do remember me – it's been more than nine years since I left Ridgely." His manner was impeccably polite, but there was no mistaking the underlying thread of steel.

"Ah – of course." The look on Rosemary's face could have curdled milk, but she didn't miss a beat; breeding will out. "How nice to see you again, Mr.Lander. Do have a pleasant evening."

"I'm sure I shall." He smiled as if completely unaware of the dismay he had stirred in the good lady's breast, and followed Annis through to the Club Room.

At least it had been a day well spent, Annis reflected as she surveyed her handiwork. Great vases of flowers, donated by the Allotment Society, were arranged around the room – lilacs and irises to pick up the soft duck-egg blue of the walls, with a bright pop of colour from the lovely yellow roses.

A long table stood at the far end, swathed with crêpe paper of the same shades, and laden with enough bottles of sparkling wine - generously donated by a cousin of Rosemary's, who imported it from Hungary - to float a battleship.

There was already quite a crowd - Ridgely wasn't the sort of town where people arrived fashionably late. Hesitating in the doorway, Annis was all too conscious of Theo's hand resting on the small of her back with a kind of casual possessiveness which conveyed the clear impression that their relationship was a good deal more intimate than it really was.

And it had been noticed, as he had intended.

Oh, no-one had the bad manners to actually be caught staring, but she was aware of their eyes, nonetheless – and aware of the discreet whispers, the ripple of scandalised speculation that followed them as they crossed the room. Her mouth felt dry, and her heart was beating a little too fast. She knew exactly what they were all saying – and it wasn't nice.

But it was no good wishing the highly-polished parquet floor would open up and swallow her. She had to go through with this – it was the price she had agreed to pay.

At least the majestic sweep of her wide silk taffeta skirt lent her an air of dignity. She held her head high as she circulated the room. Let them all think whatever they damned well liked - there was no point trying to deny anything. That would only serve to convince them even more that she had something to deny.

But for all her show of bravado, she could feel the heat of a blush in her cheeks as she was forced to introduce Theo to everyone she spoke to. By now anyone who hadn't recognised him or had forgotten the original story had been fully briefed by their friends.

But Theo had been right – being with her appeared to break down the barriers, and though some people seemed unsure how friendly they wanted to be, others seemed to be quite happy to welcome him home.

And so he had got exactly what he wanted, she reflected acidly. Many of the introductions she was making tonight could turn into valuable business contacts - all the more valuable, indeed, because of the personal touch.

But then she would guess that Theo Lander always did get what he wanted. Which left her more than a little apprehensive - because at the moment, what he wanted was her.

"Annis - hi! Hey, what a fabulous dress!" Vicky, pretty in

fuschia pink chiffon, came bouncing over, her tall handsome husband in tow. "And it's Theo Lander, isn't it?" Vicky's large brown eyes were brimming with merriment. "Vicky Bateman – Fletcher, as was. You won't remember me, of course - I was just one of the legion of silly school-girls who used to gawk over you when you were mending engines." She held out her hand. "Welcome back to Ridgely"

"Thank you." He laughed, a warm, genuine laugh, as he shook her hand, recognising her sincerity. "I'm glad to be back."

Annis felt a sharp stab of something which felt like... *jealousy*? Theo had never laughed like that with *her*. And what on earth did Vicky think she was doing, flirting with him like that, with her husband standing right behind her...

Oh, stop being so ridiculous, she chided herself impatiently - of course Vicky wasn't flirting with him. And even if she was, there was no reason for her to be the least bit bothered about it. It wasn't as if she wanted… that sort of personal relationship with him herself.

Vicky had introduced Gordon, and a chance remark about cars soon had the two men deep in conversation about the Aston Martin's powerful V12 engine. Annis took advantage of the moment to slip away.

"I'm just going to pop into the kitchen and have a word with Monsieur László," she murmured, and hurried off before Theo could stop her.

Theo was attending to the conversation with only half an ear. He was far more interested in watching Annis as she made her way across the room.

When she had opened the door tonight, she had taken his breath away. In that dress, she was stunning – the deep shade of blue was almost exactly the same colour as her eyes, and her skin glowed against it like ivory.

But not the least part of her beauty was that she seemed to treat it as being of little importance. He watched as she paused to talk to an elderly couple, giving them the whole of her attention for those few moments, then passing on smoothly to a lanky young lad still in his teens with whom she shared a joke, leaving him glowing with pleasure.

George Statham's daughter. Who would have guessed that such an evil bastard could produce such a captivating bundle of charm? She had certainly caught him - when he had been least expecting it.

Seeing the way she loved her horse, seeing her crying at the thought of losing him, had made him want to take her in his arms, kiss away the tears, promise her that nothing would ever hurt her again.

And in that reckless moment, he had waived away a considerable sum of money – and the chance to claim a house worth considerably more.

Of course, his rationale was that with access to her social network he stood a much better chance of realising his plans for regenerating the town, which could easily bring him several times that amount in profit. But if he was ruthlessly honest with himself, he had done it for one reason and one reason alone. To see her smile.

Or had she made a complete fool of him? Was she her father's daughter after all – clever, manipulative, out for the best deal no matter what she had to do to get it?

And just what *would* she do? She had vowed that her bedroom door would remain closed to him, but would she use the temptation of opening it just a chink to try to lure him deeper into her coils?

He smiled grimly to himself. He had met plenty of women like that, particularly these past few years, since his pockets had become so well-lined. If she tried that game, she would find all her aces trumped, just as her father had. But it would be very amusing to let her play out her hand.

She was still talking to someone on the far side of the room, and he allowed his gaze to linger over the creamy swell of her breasts, so enticingly showcased by the tightly-fitted basque of her dress.

Yes, very amusing.

CHAPTER FIVE

IT TOOK a while to mollify Monsieur László. "For the children I do it, for you I do it. But for that woman…" He brandished an egg-whisk threateningly in the air. "I warns you, Miss Annis - you keeps her from my kitchen, or I no be responsible for the consequences."

Having assured him that she would do her very best, Annis retreated from the kitchen, to find herself accosted by Uncle Charles. The stormy expression on his face warned her of trouble – but then she had been expecting it.

"Have you seen who's here?" he demanded, all indignant bluster. "I don't know how he has the nerve. It was bad enough that he should show up at George's funeral, but to thrust himself into a private occasion where he isn't wanted…!"

"It's hardly a private occasion, Uncle Charles," she responded carefully. "The tickets are on sale, and he bought one."

"They've never sold tickets to just anyone. There have to be certain standards. I'd like to know who permitted him to have one."

Annis drew in a deep breath. She had to tell him at some point – she might as well get it over with. "As a matter of fact it was me. And he's here with me tonight, as my guest. I do hope you won't make a scene."

She might as well have saved her breath. The old man's eyes bulged. "With you? What on earth…? Didn't I warn you to stay away from him?"

"You did. But you didn't say why."

"I'd have thought what he did to your father was reason enough! He was as good as responsible for his death – and he's disinherited you into the bargain."

"From what I can gather, it was as much my father's fault, for plunging into reckless investments, being too greedy. You can hardly blame Theo for taking advantage. Business is business - Daddy would have done exactly the same thing in his place. In fact he did, when he took advantage of Mr Lander's misfortune to buy up his land."

"His misfortune?" Uncle Charles snorted his contempt. "He was the author of his own misfortune. You talk about being too greedy! Lander was nothing but a cheap crook."

"I remember him." Annis cast her mind back to the kindly man who had always been willing to fix bicycles and baby-buggies for nothing. "I can't help thinking… Juries have been known to make mistakes…"

"Not in this case." He puffed himself up with an air of triumphant conclusion. "He pleaded guilty."

"Oh…"

"And as for the son, he's a chip off the old block. I don't know how he's managed to drag you into his coils, but you just be careful what you're doing, my girl. He's a nasty piece of work. Take it from me, there's something very fishy in all this – very fishy indeed. Don't you trust him – not as far as you could throw him."

Annis hesitated. "Well, if you really think Theo's done something criminal, perhaps we should get the police to look into it?" Why on earth did she feel an instinct to defend Theo Lander?

"No!" He seemed to realise that his sharp retort had startled her, and suddenly he was his usual avuncular self again. "No, what's done is done. You can be sure he'll have covered his tracks pretty well. It would serve no purpose - just drag it all out in public. Just you be careful, my dear – that's all I ask." He patted her hand. "It's probably a good thing to be seen to be friendly with the man in public – spike the gossips' guns. But just don't you let him spin you any lines."

She laughed. "I don't see why he'd bother. I've nothing left he'd want to steal."

But she did, she reflected bitterly. He wanted her body – she had little doubt of that. Every time he turned that wickedly sinful gaze on her she felt as if she was naked. And the problem was, she was conscious of a little thrill of excitement every time it happened.

She was close by the back door, and suddenly she really felt the need to slip outside for a few moments to breathe the cool evening air beneath the trees along the river bank.

The sky was darkening to a rich cobalt blue, streaked with lilac and indigo as the sun set. The long grass brushed damp against her toes as she walked, the soft rustling silk taffeta of her skirt whispering back to the leaves above her head as they stirred in the warm evening breeze.

Her mind was replaying that conversation with Uncle Charles. It had been a shock to hear that Theo's father had pleaded guilty. She had more-or-less convinced herself that there must have been some mistake, a miscarriage of justice. But it seemed that there was no mistake.

Even so, she still had that niggling feeling that there was something Uncle Charles hadn't told her. She had heard the rumours – that occasionally he had been known to accept a few bottles of whisky, or something a little more valuable, in return for giving a planning application a favourable consideration.

And other whispers – about whether it was quite appropriate for the cousin of one of the biggest property developers in the area to be Chairman of the Planning Committee. Was Uncle Charles afraid that if the circumstances surrounding the development of the business park were to be examined…?

A movement in the shadows made her catch her breath in shock. A tall, wide-shouldered figure appeared from beneath the trees, moving lazily, like a panther stalking his prey.

"So there you are." Theo's voice taunted her softly. "I thought you were trying to renege on our deal by slipping away before the evening had even begun."

She dragged in a few ragged breaths, all too acutely aware of the way it lifted her breasts against the taut constraint of her bodice – and all too acutely aware that he was enjoying the effect. "I... wasn't slipping away. You know I'm on the Committee. I had things to do."

"Well, you've done them now. For the rest of the evening, you don't leave my side."

"But there'll be dancing after dinner," she protested weakly.

"You can dance as much as you like. So long as you only dance with me."

"*Only* with you? But… people will talk."

"That's the general idea." He moved closer, his voice taking on a huskier timbre. "Remember? For the next few months, so far as the world at large is concerned, you're my mistress." With one finger he tilted up her chin, forcing her to look up into his eyes. "What a come-down for George Statham's high-nosed daughter - the mistress of a second-hand car salesman. And what else was it you called me? Pond life?" He was letting one fingertip trail slowly down the long, slender column of her throat. "You know, I'm going to have to punish you for that."

She felt as if she was trapped by the power of those mesmerizing eyes, unable to escape. The threat was spoken huskily, sending hot little shivers of anticipation feathering down her spine. He was challenging her to protest as his fingertip traced along the very edge of her boned bodice, across the aching swell of her breasts, as if branding her as his possession.

Those dark eyes held her captive as his hand slid down and around her waist, drawing her inexorably closer, tilting her slightly off balance so that she was curved against him, forced to put up one hand against the hard wall of his chest to steady herself.

Beneath the fine silk of his shirt she could feel the warmth of his skin against her palm, the supple movement of muscle over bone... and suddenly it was difficult to breathe.

His mouth was just a few inches from hers, their breath mingling. She knew she should draw back - she had promised herself that she wouldn't let this happen. But she knew that she had been lying to herself – she wanted him to kiss her. And as his head bent slowly over hers, her lips parted softly in invitation.

The first brush of his mouth on hers was light, tantalising, enticing her closer. Annis let her lashes drift down over her eyes as all her senses focused on the taste of Theo's kiss, the subtle male scent of his skin. She was floating, light-headed, not even sure if this was a dream.

But she wasn't dreaming that hard male body, or the strong arms that encircled her waist - and she wasn't dreaming the firm mouth that had closed over hers, the hot swirl of Theo's tongue sliding languorously over the delicate inner membranes of her lips.

Her head had tipped back as she surrendered beneath the sweet invasion, her body arched quivering against his, the stiff layers of her taffeta petticoats crushed between them, her breasts aching in their tight-boned constraint, the tender nipples ripened to exquisitely sensitised buds beneath the soft abrasion of the silk-lined bodice.

The kiss deepened as his tongue plundered all the most sensitive corners of her mouth. Annis could feel her heartbeat racing. She was clinging to him, her hands sliding up of their own volition beneath his jacket to grasp at his wide shoulders as she kissed him back, hungrily, needily, her tongue tangling sensuously with his.

Fevered images were swirling in her brain - images of lying naked in his arms in the long grass, of his hands caressing her body as she surrendered to his hungry male demands. And she knew by the ragged drag of his breathing that some strange telepathy had conveyed the message to him. *Now... Yes....*

The sound of voices, not far away, of laughter and scampering footsteps as people fooled around under the trees, brought reality rushing back like a drench of ice-water. She drew back sharply, opening her eyes in a shocked awareness of her surroundings. "Stop... Let me go." She dragged herself out of his grasp. "They'll see us."

He laughed softly, provocatively. "I told you – it's part of the deal. I want you to look convincing in your role."

Dammit - how stupid could she be? He hadn't really been engaged in the kiss at all - he had only been acting a part, while she... Struggling to ignore the flame of heat that had flared inside her, she tilted her head at a haughty angle. "I never gave you permission to kiss me."

"Then why didn't you stop me? I think we both know the

answer to that. Because for all your fine insistence about keeping the bedroom door shut, you want what you know I can give you." His voice was imbued with a promise of sinful pleasures beyond her imagination. "Though perhaps I should warn you, I like plenty of variety in the bedroom. Sometimes I prefer to make love long, slow and comfortable, and sometimes I like it sweaty and raw. And I'd expect nothing less than total compliance."

Annis closed her eyes for a brief moment, conjuring every ounce of willpower she possessed to resist the treacherous weakness inside her which was all too ready to surrender to anything he demanded. "Whatever." She shrugged her slim shoulders in a dismissive gesture. "If you ask me, sex is very much over-rated."

He arched one dark eyebrow in amused question. "You think so?"

"All that stupid orgasm stuff." She forced herself to meet his eyes in cool defiance. "It's all just made up to sell magazines."

"You mean you've never had an orgasm?" He stared at her, laughing in open incredulity. "Oh, come on - you don't seriously expect me to believe that?"

Dammit, why had she said that? She might have known he would only mock her. "Believe what you like," she threw back at him, stung. "It's true."

He shook his head as if in sorrow, though a taunting smile still lingered at the corners of his firm mouth. "Well, I suppose it's hardly surprising, if your experience to date is with the likes of Jerry Cummings. But it certainly presents a challenge – one I don't think any red-blooded man could resist."

"Don't hold your breath."

"Oh, I don't think I shall have to wait too long." His voice was husky with sensuous promise. "And when you come to my bed, you'll find out that orgasms aren't just made up to sell magazines."

Annis felt the heat shimmer through her. A small voice inside her was whispering that he was right – or at least that it would be very interesting to find out. But pride wouldn't let her concede the point.

From somewhere she found the strength to pull away from him, retreating behind her facade of icy dignity. "Like I said, don't hold your breath." And turning him an aloof shoulder she stalked away, bristling with haughty disdain.

Unfortunately the effect was somewhat marred as she caught the slim heel of her sandals in a crack between the pavers on the terrace outside the club house. Off balance, she almost fell, but Theo's arm slid around her waist again.

"Remember what I said." There was a soft hint of menace in his voice. "I want this to look convincing. You're with me, and you stay with me the whole evening. Is that clear?"

Her jaw clamped on the fury welling up inside her. Yes, it was clear. He was treating her like a possession. But she really had no right to object - she had agreed to his terms. Which left her with two options - she could sulk, or she could sparkle. People were going to gossip either way, and on the whole she would prefer if they did it on the basis of the latter.

Freeing her foot, she conjured her most brilliant smile and stepped back into the fray.

Everyone agreed that it was a wonderful supper - Monsieur László had excelled himself. A delicious sea-food roulade, tangy with lemon and ginger, was followed by tender breast of duck with pears and a potpourri of spicy vegetables, and a desert of delicate cappuccino parfait served in individual dark chocolate cups, swirled with whipped cream and chocolate flakes.

Theo had declined the sweet and moved straight to the coffee. Annis was giving him no reason to complain, he reflected wryly. She was as sparking as the wine, laughing and chatting with the other guests who shared their table, most of whom were apparently old friends. No-one would have guessed for a moment that she was anything less than joyously happy with the man at her side.

So why did he feel such a sharp niggle of frustration?

Perhaps because she was putting on *such* a good act. How much had been an act that day up at the house, when her tears for her horse had called on his sympathy? How much had been an act outside beneath the shadow of the trees earlier this evening?

The memory of that moment helped him pin-point more precisely the source of his irritation. He was sick of sitting here making polite conversation with people who almost certainly despised him. He wanted to get Annis on her own again, feel her soft, supple body in his arms, caress that smooth, creamy skin, savour the anticipation as her resistance warred with her unmistakable desire to surrender.

Which meant that it was probably fortunate that he was sitting down.

A slight prickle at the back of his neck made him suspect that someone was looking at him. Half turning his head, he noticed Sir Charles Statham sitting several tables away from them, his sour glare endangering the fizz in the sparkling wine.

A man with something to hide. He deliberately allowed a small smile to curve his mouth as he returned the older man's gaze. It would be very interesting to know what it was.

He noticed with a sinking heart that Rosemary Trenchard had risen to her feet and was tinkling her knife against her glass to call for attention. Speeches, votes of thanks… He stifled a yawn, easing a little closer to Annis's side, lifting his arm to rest it across the back of her chair, letting his fingers toy idly with a soft tendril of hair that had slipped down from that fetching little up-do and was curling over the nape of her neck.

She moved restively, those enticingly round breasts crushing against the taut-boned cups of her bodice. At least he had something to entertain him while he sat through the parade of the great and good of the town, he mused with a touch of wicked amusement – and all the more so because he could tell by the faint blush of pink in her cheeks that she knew exactly what he was looking at.

Annis could feel herself growing hot. The brush of Theo's

fingertips on her the back of her neck was so light, like a butterfly's wing, but it was sending sizzling little sparks of electricity down her spine. And with every ragged breath she was breathing the subtle male scent of him, a scent that was doing crazy things to her pulse-rate.

His mistress… He was right – for all the warnings from the rational part of her mind, her body wanted him. The flickering flame of the candle in the middle of their table had drawn her gaze, as images swirled in her head… images of him watching her with those mesmerising dark eyes…

"Take off your clothes…" Moving with a fluid grace like the flame of the candle, she obeyed, unfastening the zip of her dress and letting it fall to the floor, where it pooled like a wave of blue silk around her ankles. Naked except for a pair of tiny white lace briefs and a pair of high-heeled silver sandals, she stood in front of him as he let his eyes wander over every inch of her body.

He smiled slowly.

"Take down your hair." His voice was huskily soft. She lifted her hands to the clips, the movement lifting her small breasts invitingly, the dainty pink peaks hardening to tender nubs as she swayed towards him, ready to surrender to his every demand…

"And of course our dear Annis, who has worked so hard again this year to make the room so lovely," she heard Rosemary's voice announce, and suddenly she was the focus of every eye in the room, people were clapping politely.

She was aware that her cheeks were a deep scarlet as she rose briefly to her feet to acknowledge the applause. At least they would all assume that her flustered state was caused by finding herself the centre of attention – no one could know that it was caused by the shock of being jerked so abruptly out of a very steamy fantasy.

At last the formal part of the evening was over. The tables began to empty as people drifted back to the Club Room, where a five-piece band had started playing an old Beatles hit on the small stage.

"Shall we…?" Theo held out his hand, indicating with a

77

nod the direction the others had taken.

Annis allowed him to take her hand and draw her to her feet.

He leaned across to the flower centre-piece of their table, and pulled out a half-opened yellow rose, and slipped it into his buttonhole. Then he took another, lifting it to breathe in the sweet scent.

"Beautiful…" And turning to her, he tucked it into the top of her dress so that it nestled in the soft valley between her breasts like a jewel. "Beautiful."

Annis stared up at him, not quite sure what to say. From anyone else, she may have thought it was a romantic gesture. But from Theo Lander it felt… possessive – as if she wore a token that marked her out as exclusively his.

It hadn't been too difficult sitting next to him through supper, with three other couples at their table to diffuse the tension between them. But now there would be dancing – which would give him an excuse to wrap those strong arms around her again, hold her body close against his.

You can dance as much as you like – so long as you only dance with me.

Her mouth felt suddenly dry.

The lights had all been dimmed in the Club Room, leaving only the colourful display behind the band on the stage. A few people were already dancing; most were topping up their wine glasses or standing around easing well-fed stomachs and chatting with friends they hadn't spoken to for… oh, at least an hour.

Annis circulated dutifully – listening with interest to the latest news of Glenys Johnson's new grand-daughter, asking after Jim Roberts' prize begonias. But all the time she was acutely aware of the man at her side, of the way his arm loosely encircled her waist.

Her mind struggled to think of some excuse to escape early, but nothing presented itself – her brain seemed to have turned to mush.

They had just finished speaking to the new vicar of the

Methodist church, who had been keen to engage her help with their Summer Fête, when Vicky came bouncing up.

"Hey, come on!" She grabbed Annis's hand. "What are you doing standing around? They're playing a Stones medley - we should be dancing!"

Annis hesitated. "I don't know. I was just thinking I ought to get home. The horses…"

"Oh, they'll be fine for one evening," Vicky insisted blithely. "I'm your vet, and I'm telling you that it's time to party!"

Somehow Annis managed to keep her smile in place and allowed herself to be dragged away, though she could cheerfully have rung her exuberant friend's neck. In a flurry of rustling petticoats she was swept into the middle of the crowded dance-floor.

The music was loud and lively, compelling her to dance. She had half-hoped that she had left Theo behind, at least for a while. She couldn't quite him imagine him getting down-and-dirty to a blast of old-fashioned rock'n'roll. Especially when he could use the opportunity instead to schmooze a few more business contacts.

But he was there behind her, slipping his arm around her waist, a wicked smile curving his hard mouth. "You hadn't forgotten, had you?" His voice was a purr, menacingly soft. "You're dancing only with me."

She turned to him with eyes that sparkled just a little too brightly. If she couldn't win one way, perhaps she could win in another. "Of course." She smiled sweetly. "Do you jive?" Now let him see – she would dance him into the ground.

A vain hope that was, she reflected a couple of hours later as he still showed no sign of flagging. The most he had done was take off his jacket and unfasten his bow-tie, leaving it loose around the open collar of his shirt, which gave her a tantalising glimpse of that dark shadow of hair curling at the base of his throat.

He moved well, easy on the rhythm, neither stiff and embarrassed like ninety percent of the men, nor jerking himself around like a wooden puppet with half its strings missing, like most of the remainder.

It was coming on for midnight, and the crowd was beginning to thin a little. At last the music changed to a slower, more romantic melody, and Theo slid his arm around her waist, drawing her closer against him. For a moment she stiffened in instinctive resistance, but he laughed softly, his grip tightening just enough to warn her that she was still his prisoner.

"You don't think I'm going to let you run away now, do you?" he taunted.

For a moment she thought of protesting, of suggesting that perhaps they should go up to the bar for a drink instead. But he was holding her very close, moving her to the hypnotic rhythms, his thigh hard against hers, his warm breath stirring her hair.

And with every breath she took, the subtle male scent of his skin was inveigling her senses like a drug — a highly addictive drug. She would pull away in a moment, she promised herself weakly.

But first… just this one dance…

There was a hunger inside her, consuming her, drawing her ever deeper into the web of temptation he was spinning around her. Dancing in his arms, her body moving with his as the romantic strains of the music drifted around them, she knew that it was her will he held captive as much as her body.

If she wasn't very careful, he could make her fall in love with him.

One dance, then another, and another. Time had no meaning – she could go on dancing like this for ever… It was only when Theo murmured softly in her ear, "I think we'd better call it a night," that she realised that the band had stopped playing and were starting to pack up their instruments, the lights had gone up.

Annis drew back, suddenly conscious of the cool night air on her bare shoulders now that she was no longer absorbed in the warmth of his body. She had never meant to let herself get so carried away.

And so he had won another victory – she had danced with him, and only him, all night, just as he had demanded.

And she knew by the glint of amusement in his dark eyes that he was taunting her with that fact.

There were only a few couples left in the Club Room, yawning as they gathered up their handbags and jackets. A couple of half-deflated balloons were drifting across the duckboard dance-floor, some of the paper garlands had fallen down across the chairs, and a faint smell of sweaty bodies and stale alcohol permeated the air.

Annis laughed a little edgily, trying to regain some semblance of normality. She glanced around at the debris left behind. "Oh dear, this is going to take hours to clear up."

"You're surely not planning to do that tonight?" Theo protested, startled.

She shook her head. "Oh no – there's a bunch of sixth-formers from the high school coming in to help tomorrow morning. But I ought to go and say thank you to everyone who's helped out tonight – if they're still here."

She had done little herself, she reflected with a small twinge of guilt - Theo had only insisted that she shouldn't dance with anyone else, not that she had to dance all evening with him.

But dancing with him had meant that she could be in his arms... And no-one had made the slightest move to cut in on them. That thought brought a slight blush of pink to her cheeks; they must have been giving off a very powerful message.

Theo nodded assent. "I'll wait for you in the bar."

To take her home. And then...? Did he expect that she would invite him in – 'for coffee'? And if he took that as a coded invitation for something more, would she be able to resist him?

Rosemary was back at her post in the entrance hall, her face now a little shiny but flushed with triumph - and maybe the effects of a glass or several of sparkling wine. "A brilliant evening! We've raised more money than ever before. Thank you – you've been wonderful, simply wonderful."

Annis found herself almost crushed in a leaf-green bear-hug, but she smiled in private amusement. It was the same every year, after all the fretting and angst.

"And your friend Mr Lander. Such a generous cheque. I must say I never expected it from him. But then after all, we really shouldn't blame him for what his father did. And so sensible of you, my dear, to have allowed him to take over your father's company. Men are so much better at business than we women are – my father always said so."

Annis concealed her surprise. Who had spun that little story? Theo? Well, it probably suited both of them if people thought that was the way it had been, she conceded. Annoyed as she was with her father, she really didn't want people knowing the whole sorry saga.

Turning her head just slightly she could see him sitting on a stool at the end of the bar, a drink in his hand - talking to someone. Someone with bottle-blonde highlights in her artfully rumpled, come-to-bed hair.

Lucinda Forsyth. Annis vaguely recalled seeing her earlier with Rosemary's son Crispin – he was now slumped in a chair in the corner, looking rather the worse for drink. Not that Lucy seemed to care - she was too busy fluttering her fake eyelashes at Theo. As Annis watched, she touched his arm lightly with her flashily-manicured fingertips.

A sudden burning desire to march over there and douse the little madam's sparkle with the business end of a fire extinguisher took her by surprise.

Dammit - she was *jealous!*

Oh, wouldn't that make Theo laugh, if he should guess. Which meant she was going to have to make damned sure he didn't find out, she vowed resolutely. Turning her back, she refused to allow herself to look in his direction again. But her smile was a little brittle, her laughter a little too loud as the last of the guests drifted away.

Nearly everyone had gone - but Theo was still talking to the lovely Lucinda. Annis hesitated, unsure what to do. She certainly didn't want to have to go over and interrupt, like some kind of supplicant for the crumbs of his attention. But she didn't want to appear to be waiting for him, either.

Her knight in shining armour appeared in the unexpected

form of Jeremy Cummings. "Jerry – I thought you'd left."

Jeremy ran his hand back through his floppy fringe in a characteristically boyish gesture. "I did. But m'sister forgot her jacket, and absolutely insisted that I had to come back for it. Don't know why – could just have easily have fetched the stupid thing in the morning, but there you go. It was easier to give in than to argue with her."

Annis caught his arm, casting a swift glance back over her shoulder. "Jerry, could you give me a lift home?" she pleaded urgently. "My... taxi hasn't shown up."

He smiled his slightly vacuous smile. "Oh - yes of course, old girl. Happy to oblige. But I thought you were with Lander?" he added with a befuddled frown.

"I... was with him earlier, but he... had to leave." She drew Jeremy to one side so that he couldn't see into the club-room. "He's got an early flight to America tomorrow. I'll just get my wrap."

She darted into the cloakroom, snatched up her Pashmina and darted out again, grabbing a somewhat bemused Jeremy by the arm and dragging him out to the car-park. "I'm in rather a hurry to get home," she explained. "I need to make sure the horses are OK."

"Oh... of course." He led the way to his car - a low-slung Italian sports job with racy lines and not much room inside. Annis frowned - how would she get her skirt into it without getting it sadly crushed? But then the ball was over - she could have it dry cleaned before she needed to wear it again.

If she ever did need to wear it again. It probably wasn't very wise to let her reckless pride make the decisions, but she would *not* let Theo Lander humiliate her. If he decided to punish her for leaving without him by calling off the deal, well... so be it.

She swallowed hard. If he did, never having the occasion to wear extravagant ball-gowns again would be the least of her problems.

Maybe she ought to go back inside…

No, dammit, she would *not* crawl to him. Jeremy had opened the car door for her, and she settled herself a little awkwardly into the passenger seat, tucking her knees to one side to make room for the rustling taffeta of her skirt.

But just as Jeremy was about to climb in beside her, the door was wrenched open again, and a familiar voice drawled, "Ah - there you are." A hand closed around her wrist like a steel vice, hauling her to feet, and she found herself gazing up into a pair of dangerous dark eyes. "You must have had more to drink than I realised if you'd forgotten I was taking you home."

CHAPTER SIX

ANNIS snatched her wrist out of Theo's grasp. "You know I'm not drunk!" she hissed.

He laughed indulgently, putting on an act worthy of an Oscar. "Oh, not drunk, perhaps, but certainly a little well-to-go." His smile warned her not to argue. "Thanks, Jeremy old chap, but we won't need to put you to the trouble after all. Come along, darling. Whoops..." He had nudged her sharply in the back of the knees so that she staggered slightly, appearing to give the proof to his implication that she had had too many glasses of wine. "Careful." He slipped his arm around her waist, pinning her to his side. "We don't want you to end up falling over in a ditch, do we?"

Her violet blue eyes flashed him a fulminating glare, but there was nothing she could do - his arm around her was forcing her to walk with him to his car. If she tried to escape, it would just cause a scene – and she had stirred up enough scandal for one night. He opened the door of the Aston Martin, pushing her down into the passenger seat and tucking her skirt in around her.

"Damn you, I can manage." Angrily she knocked his hands away.

He laughed, and strolled round the front of the car to slip into the driver's seat beside her. "I did warn you not to try to run away," he reminded her, gunning the engine and reversing the car smoothly out of its parking space.

"You have no right to do this," she seethed.

"You came with me, you leave with me." There was an unmistakeable thread of steel in his voice. "That's the way it goes, or the deal's off."

His ruthless reminder chilled her to the bone. But she had known the score when she had accepted his terms, she reminded herself bitterly – from that moment, she had sacrificed her freedom for the next six months.

She had no choice but to accept his every demand – a position which felt more humiliating than if she really had been his mistress. She just had to keep telling herself that it would be worth it, to buy herself the time to save her home and her horses.

"Anyway, you appeared to be busy," she retorted with dignity, tilting up her chin and turning to gaze out of the window as they drove out of the car-park.

"You mean Lucy?"

Annis felt her jaw tense. "You seemed to be very friendly with her."

"You sound jealous."

"Not in the least. It's entirely your own affair."

He laughed softly. "Oh, I don't know that you could call it an affair, though I did go out with her a few times, way back when."

"You've slept with her?" Damn - what demon had taken over her tongue?

He slanted her a smile of mocking reproof. "Now that's not a very ladylike question."

She shrugged her slender shoulders in a gesture of cool dismissal. "I really couldn't care less if you did or not."

"So why did you ask?"

Annis's mouth thinned. She was furious with him for goading her, and furious with herself for falling into so easy a trap.

With an impatient gesture she snatched the yellow rose from her cleavage, intending to crush it under her heel. But it was much too beautiful to destroy.

Theo laughed softly, as if he knew exactly what was running through her mind. "Would you really have preferred to go home with Jeremy? You know you'll have much more fun with me."

"*Fun*…?" She imbued the word with as much contempt as she dared.

"Would Jeremy make love to you on silk sheets, with your wrists tied to the bed-posts so he could torment your naked body with pleasure until you were begging for mercy?" His voice was huskily soft, conjuring up the vivid image his words were painting. "Or in the lift of a five-star hotel, with only his finger on the button to stop the doors from opening? He probably never even makes love with the lights on…"

"Stop it." Her cheeks had flamed scarlet. "I told you, I'm not going to…

"Sleep with me?"

"Yes! I mean… no."

"Never?"

"Never."

And turning her head away again, she stared out of the window at the dark world passing outside, refusing to look at him or speak to him all the rest of the way home.

The security lights along the drive came on as Theo turned the car between the stone gate-posts. Annis had already released her seat-belt as he brought the car to a stop with a soft crunch of gravel in front of the house, intending to be out of her seat and away before he could detain her. But in her haste she caught her stupid heel in her voluminous petticoats, and was still struggling to free it as he opened the passenger door.

"Allow me."

He lifted the hem, his fingers brushing lightly against her ankle as he unhooked the rustling taffeta from her shoe. An odd little shiver of heat ran through her. In an earlier age, she reflected, it would have been considered quite scandalous for a man to touch her ankle.

These days, of course, it meant absolutely nothing. Not even when his hand lingered, sliding tantalisingly up over the smooth skin of her calf. Absolutely nothing at all...

"You have no reason to be jealous of Lucy Forsyth." Those dark eyes glinted with amusement – and something more. "You know you were the most beautiful woman in the place tonight."

Her heart fluttered like a trapped butterfly. The most beautiful woman in the place… It was nonsense, of course – just the sort of thing a man would say to a woman he was planning to seduce. Only an idiot would let herself believe he meant it.

"I wasn't jealous."

"Yes you were." He took both her hands in his, drawing

her easily to her feet but keeping her trapped against the side of the car. "You wanted to know if I'd slept with her. You were wondering how often, whether it had been good. Whether I would think it was better with you."

"Don't be ridiculous." That frosty facade was her only defence against him. "I told you, I'm not... I'm not going to..."

He was ignoring her protests. Instead he had slid one hand along the delicate line of her jaw, tilting her face up to his. "I know. You told me. Several times. Which leaves me wondering…" He bent his head, dusting a trail of light, hot kisses over her eyelids as they trembled shut. "…who you're trying to convince of that – me, or yourself."

"I'm not… going to sleep with you..." Her voice was no more than a ragged whisper as with a soft, helpless sigh her lips parted beneath his, giving the lie to her words.

"When you come to my bed…" His breath was warm against her cheek. "I doubt that either of us will do much sleeping."

His kiss was deep and sensual, sweeping languorously into all the sweet, secret corners of her mouth. His strong arms were wrapped around her, crushing her close against him, conveying the unmistakable warning that with very little effort he could make her do whatever he wanted. She could feel herself weakening against that treacherous undertow of temptation.

It would be so easy...

As if he sensed her faltering resistance, he lifted his head, a glint of lazy amusement in his dark eyes. "So, are we just going to kiss goodnight out here on the doorstep like a couple of horny adolescents, or are you going to invite me in?"

"No..."

Somehow the rational part of her mind was still struggling to hold onto the scattered threads of her sanity. If she gave in, she would surrender every last shred of her dignity. She would become his plaything - was that what she wanted? She shook her head, resolutely ignoring the treacherous part of her mind which was whispering the suggestion that to be Theo Lander's plaything might not be all bad.

"That wasn't part of the deal. If you've changed your mind about trying to coerce me into sleeping with you…"

His hand lifted to her cheek, his finger coiling in a straying strand of hair that had fallen from the barrette keeping it in place. "Oh, I don't think I shall need to coerce you." He still had her trapped against the side of the car, the unyielding barrier of his arm making it abundantly clear that she wasn't going to be able to escape until he chose to let her go. "I think when the time comes, you'll be very willing indeed."

She was struggling to keep her breathing even, far too aware of how every movement lifted the creamy round swell of her breasts and crushed them taut against the tight-boned cups of her silk bodice, the tender peaks sizzling against the soft abrasion of the silk lining.

A faint smile creased the corners of his hard mouth as he let his dark eyes linger over the ripe curves, as if picturing in his imagination their nakedness, warm and inviting, pertly tipped with nipples the sweet, deep pink of ripe raspberries.

"You know, if you really want me to believe you've never had an orgasm, you really shouldn't respond so delightfully whenever I touch you."

With one finger he traced the line of the boned seam, up from her slender waist, and slowly up over the round curve of her breast. A hot shimmer of anticipation feathered down her spine.

He bent his head close to her ear. "You see what I mean?" His voice was soft and smoky. "I only have to look at you for you to catch fire."

She knew it was true - but there wasn't a thing she could do about it. His breath was hot against the delicate shell of her ear, his sensuous tongue finding an exquisitely sensitive spot just behind her lobe and tracing a sizzling path down the long, slender column of her throat, to linger in the hollow of her shoulder, where a rapid pulse fluttered beneath her smooth skin.

Then his mouth moved to claim hers again, demanding nothing less than her total surrender, and she had no defences left. Imprisoned against the side of the car, she could only part her lips beneath the marauding invasion, yielding all the dark, moist territories of her mouth to the flagrantly sensual exploration of his tongue.

If only time really could stand still; if only he would go on kissing her like this forever, with this deep, tender intimacy. His mistress... making love on silk sheets... *Aren't you tempted?* a soft, insidious voice was whispering inside her head. *Just surrender...*

His kiss was sweet and erotic, the swirling plunder of his tongue and the smooth caress of his hand on her aching breast a presage of the intimate possession he was luring her towards...

No! Don't be a fool! Some rational corner of her mind was still clinging to a shred of sanity. This was just part of his cruel game. Her father had cheated him of the full measure of his revenge by dying, and so he was taking it out on her instead. If she let herself believe it meant anything to him, she would end up getting her heart broken.

But her heart was refusing to hear the warning - or maybe it just didn't want to know.

At long last Theo lifted his head, his smile taunting her as she stared up at him with wide, dazed eyes. "Yes, you want me to make love to you. But there's still that hint of hesitation. When you come to my bed, I want you totally willing. Maybe you need a little longer to think it over."

And before she had time to recover her senses he had moved her away from the car and closed the door. Strolling around to the other side, he paused before climbing in behind the wheel. "I'll be in touch."

Without another word he slid into the car, and as she watched, he gunned the powerful engine and swung away with a crunch of the tyres over gravel - leaving her standing alone in the middle of the drive, shredding that stupid yellow rose with trembling fingers as she watched the red tail lights of the Aston Martin disappear into the night.

♥

"And so if we examine the figures for the past five

years… You'll see I've represented them in graph form…"

Wearily Theo turned over the page to study the little rows of shaded columns, failing to summon the least enthusiasm for trying to work out what they all meant.

Why on earth had he agreed to a meeting with his Senior Sales Analyst and his Chief Accountant for first thing on a Monday morning? In fact why had he agreed to meet with them at all? He should have just let them get on with it between them, and report the gist of it to him afterwards.

After all, the company was getting too big now for him to keep his finger on every button. Judicious delegation, that was what he needed to practice. Give himself time for other things - maybe even time just to enjoy himself.

A holiday, maybe - somewhere seriously hot. With a beautiful companion… a companion with hair the colour of golden honey, and wearing nothing but a very, very skimpy black bikini…

"I don't think the cost-benefit ratio really justifies that sort of conclusion - do you, Theo?"

He looked up abruptly, surprised to realise how far he had been letting his mind wander. Dammit, this was beginning to happen rather too often lately. He would be trying to concentrate on something completely different, and the image of the eminently desirable Miss Statham would somehow intrude itself into his brain.

"I'd like to hear Helen's rationale for her recommendations." Hopefully that piece of blandly neutral management-speak would disguise the fact that he hadn't been listening to a word. He really must try to pay attention, he reminded himself forcefully - though it would have helped if it wasn't all so damned tedious…

The thought of that tempting body in a tiny bikini… Now that was much more interesting. Absently twirling his pencil between his fingers, he let his mind drift again.

With that delicate ivory skin, she would need to wear plenty of sun-cream, of course - and he would be more than willing to help her rub it in… Stroking his hands up over those long, slim thighs, that slender midriff… slipping off her bikini top so that it wouldn't leave white marks… smoothing the cream over her invitingly naked breasts, small and firm like ripe peaches, tipped with tender pink nipples which puckered beneath his touch like sweet summer raspberries...

Why had she claimed that she had never had an orgasm? It seemed most unlikely – she generated enough sexual electricity to light up a small town. It was all just part of that game she played, the Ice-Princess act.

He almost laughed aloud, suppressing it quickly as he did his best to pretend he was listening to the discussion across the table.

If she thought she could play games with him, she would find out pretty quickly that he wasn't one of those Hooray Henrys she met at her swanky London parties. And teaching her that lesson could be a lot of fun...

The pencil between his fingers snapped abruptly, startling everyone around the table. "I'm... sorry Theo." His Chief Accountant was looking at him a little anxiously. "Is there something wrong with the figures?"

"No, no - carry on." He encouraged the man to continue with a wave of his hand, putting the two halves of the pencil down carefully at the top of his blotter. Damn the woman - why did he keep letting her occupy his thoughts like this?

She was George Statham's daughter, for goodness sake. Why would he want to have anything to do with her? He ought to have let his legal people evict her without any more ado - that was all she deserved.

Although… she hadn't turned out to be quite the rich bitch he had expected her to be, he reflected. There was something about her - a kind of sparkle. He had watched her at the Charity Ball on Saturday night, charming everybody with that dazzling smile, seemingly genuinely interested in everyone she spoke to.

But then of course girls from her kind of background were taught how to do that as an essential part of their education, he reminded himself caustically. It meant nothing - like doing her bit for the Friends of the Hospice committee. It was simply what was expected.

Anyway, he didn't have to like her to bed her, he reminded himself harshly - the physical attraction would more than suffice. And the sooner the better. Maybe then she wouldn't be quite so much of a distraction.

Sleep with her, and let the thing run its course - a few weeks, a few months at most. Then part on friendly terms. That was the usual pattern of his affairs - he could see no reason why this one should be any different.

Except that it *was* different, he was forced to acknowledge with a quirk of wry honesty. He wanted a lot more than just to make love to her. He wanted to drag her down off her high horse, force her to beg him to be allowed to be his mistress. The mistress of a second hand car salesman - pond life, even.

He smiled slowly to himself, almost tasting the anticipation. It had started out as a kind of game, that mistress thing - a form of retaliation for her haughty disdain. But now it had become a challenge.

Of course, he held the mortgage on her house. Not that he would ever resort to holding that over her head, except maybe to taunt her a little - a hint of reluctance could be amusing.

But it wouldn't be necessary to coerce her anyway, he reflected - the way she had responded to his kisses told him all that he needed to know. She was on the brink – it would take very little to lure her into total surrender.

And then she was going to pay for every single insult she had thrown at him.

♥

The roses were yellow. A vibrant golden yellow, with a lick of orange flame in their heart. The same yellow as the rose he had given her on Saturday night. Annis stood with them in her arms as she closed the door on the florist's delivery boy.

There was no card, but she didn't need one - she knew who they were from. Only one man would send her such fabulous yellow roses.

She ought to dump them straight in the dustbin, she chided herself crossly. She ought to have told the delivery boy to take them straight back. But she couldn't do it – they were much too beautiful to throw away.

He knew that, of course – that was why he had sent them.

He knew that she would have to put them in a vase, to look at them every time she passed the door of the sitting room. Knew that their heavenly fragrance would fill the whole house.

Very clever. He intended them to be a constant reminder of Saturday night, of the way they had danced together, the way he had kissed her. As if she was able to forget about him for more than a whole minute at a time.

She carried the flowers into the kitchen and set them down on the draining board while she searched for a vase. Her phone hadn't rung... She pulled it from her pocket and checked for missed calls.

Nothing.

How long would he leave it before he rang? No doubt demanding that she cancel everything else in order to suit his schedule. Well, she would just have to come up with some kind of plausible excuse.

But he didn't ring. Of course she wasn't checking call list half-a-dozen times an hour – it was just that someone else might ring, maybe about one of the horses – well, that was what she told herself.

But he didn't ring. Instead, each morning came another bunch of roses – the same beautiful long-stemmed yellow variety. How had he known that she loved yellow roses? By Friday she was running out of places to put them – there were two large vases in the sitting room, one in the dining room, one in the hall...

She was just finishing arranging the latest delivery, placing them carefully to show them off to their best advantage, when the phone rang.

"Ouch...!"

She was so on edge that the sound had made her jump, and she had pricked her thumb on a sharp thorn. Sucking at the oozing drip of blood, she pulled it from her pocket and checked the screen. Maggie. Her father's… No, *Theo's* secretary.

She closed her eyes for a moment, refusing to acknowledge the tiny stab of disappointment in her heart.

"Hi Maggie."

"Hello Annis - how are you?"

"I'm fine – and you?"

"Absolutely great!" The older woman's voice was buoyant with enthusiasm. "I got a lovely big pay-rise, and we're having the office done up at last. Theo's the best boss I've ever…" She cut herself off abruptly. "Oh, I'm sorry. I didn't mean to imply…"

"No, that's OK, Maggie - you deserve a pay rise. And if he's getting rid of all that awful fake Victoriana he has my vote."

"I'm afraid I did always think it was a bit over-the-top," Maggie confided. "It was like working in some fusty old museum. I like nice bright colours - Theo said I can pick my own paint for my office."

"That's very nice of him." *So he had to resort to buying off his staff with a tin of paint?*

"Anyway, he asked me to ring and confirm that you're free to have lunch with him today. He suggested that you come down to the office for twelve-thirty – he said to tell you he's sorry that he can't pick you up, but he has meetings all morning. Will that be convenient?"

Annis drew in a long, deep breath, forcing down the rising surge of annoyance. *Will that be convenient?* As if he cared a fig for her convenience. It simply wouldn't be a consideration for him - if she had had any plans for the day, he would just have told her to cancel them.

She was tempted to plead a sudden dose of the flu, but she had little doubt that he would come round and drag her out of bed.

"Yes... Um... that's fine, Maggie," she conceded tautly. "Twelve-thirty. Thanks for ringing."

"Good. I'll see you later then. Goodbye."

"Goodbye."

Annis cut the call and pulled a face at the phone. Damn the man. This was no doubt what she could expect – he would snap his fingers, and she would be expected to jump to his command. He probably treated all his mistresses that way.

His mistress...

For a moment she closed her eyes, letting the images flood her mind. Hot, fevered images that made the blood swirl in her veins – images of that lean, hard, male body naked on hers, his strong hands caressing her, sliding down over her aching breasts, her smooth stomach, between her slim thighs...

Dammit, he was right. She wanted him.

The trouble was, although he had made it quite clear that he wanted her, she knew that they had very different aims. For her, it could never remain a purely physical thing. She wanted the long-term, the meaning, the commitment – while what he wanted was a convenient mistress, merely someone who would be compliant in his bed.

Until he got bored, and his fickle fancy moved on.

♥

Annis turned off the roundabout and into the car-park outside what had once been her father's office. It was another blisteringly hot summer's day, and she had driven with the roof down. Even that short distance had left her hair wildly tousled, and she paused to drag a comb through it, then took a deep steadying breath before marching up to the front entrance.

Jill was at the reception desk, and she greeted her with a breezy smile as she crossed to the lift. She had no idea why Theo had wanted her to come into the office, and she hadn't known what to wear.

In the end she had settled for a casually elegant outfit of cool cream linen slacks teamed with a simple sleeveless shirt in apricot-coloured twisted silk, her trademark chain-link belt slung below her slender waist – this one was of cleverly-carved wooden links. It was far too hot to wear much in the way of make-up – just a touch of mascara on her lashes and a hint of gloss on her lips.

The decorators were already at work on the top floor. The ugly Victorian prints had gone from the walls, and a paint-spattered sheet covered the floor all along the corridor, where a couple of men in boiler-suits were singing along to the radio as they rollered white paint onto the ceiling.

Annis stepped carefully past the step-ladder and opened the door to Maggie's office. The secretary was sitting at her desk – a new light-wood one, with a new large-screen LED monitor. She looked up with a glowing smile as Annis entered. "Hi Annis – lovely to see you. I'll just tell Theo…"

But before she could reach for the intercom button the far door opened, and Theo himself appeared, looking cool and relaxed with the jacket of his pale grey business suit hooked casually over one shoulder, his white cotton shirt open at the throat and folded back at the cuffs.

It was crazy, but every time she saw him Annis felt her heart give an odd little jolt – there was something so essentially male about him that she just couldn't help responding to.

He greeted her with a wide, welcoming and totally insincere smile. "Incredible – a woman who doesn't keep me waiting! I knew you were unique the moment I met you."

He caught her around the waist before she could evade him, drawing her against him with a sharp jerk that almost pulled her off her feet, forcing her to put her hands up against his chest to steady herself – and then took ruthless advantage of the small gasp of surprise that parted her lips to claim her mouth in a kiss that must have looked hot enough to ignite the papers on Maggie's desk.

"Did you get my flowers?" he asked as he finally let her go.

"Yes… Thank you." Her smile was taut, and didn't reach her eyes. "They were lovely."

"Good." He kept his arm around her waist as he led her through the door, tossing a casual, "Bye, Maggie – see you later," over his shoulder.

As they walked back along the corridor to the lift, Annis struggled to regain some composure – which wasn't easy when her lips were still tingling from the heat of his kiss. "Thank you – you can let me go now," she hissed, struggling to free herself from his grip.

"Oh no." He bent his head close to her ear, as if murmuring sweet nothings. "I want office gossip – lots of it. So smile."

As if on cue, a door opened and a couple of people from the technical drawing office appeared - people she had known for years. "Annis – hi!" they greeted her, stepping back to allow her and Theo to pass, their expressions conveying amused interest at the sight of the two of them together.

Office gossip…

"Satisfied?"

His eyes glinted with wicked amusement. "It's a start."

"Presumably there's some purpose to all this play-acting?"

"Of course. It didn't take me five minutes to pick up that all the staff here think the world of you. So if I want them on my side, I need them to believe that *you're* on my side – just as much as the great and good in the town."

Annis almost had to laugh – he was the most exasperating man! There really was no way to get the better of him. "So you're expanding my job description?" A touch of light humour was probably the best way to handle this. "Perhaps I should demand better terms in our contract?"

He laughed that soft, husky laugh that always did strange things to her pulse-rate. He pressed the call-button for the lift. As the doors opened he ushered her in, his hand slipping from her waist to mould over the smooth curve of her derrière.

"I'm always willing to negotiate a change in the terms." He leaned close, his breath warm on the nape of her neck.

With a sudden thud of alarm she remembered what he had said about making love to her in the lift of a five-star hotel. This wasn't a hotel, but it was a lift… Moving quickly away from him to the far side of the tiny cabin, she leaned back against the wall, her arms crossed defensively across her chest.

"Do you always get your secretary to arrange your dates?" she challenged boldly.

"Only if I suspect that the young lady in question might find some excuse to avoid it."

"Does that happen often?"

He quirked his lips, slanting his eyes up as if trying to recall. "Hmmm… Now I come to think about it, no it doesn't."

Annis had to suppress a smile. She couldn't deny that he had a sense of humour, though mostly it was well-hidden beneath that arrogant exterior. She was going to have to be very careful to keep herself from slipping under his spell.

She dragged in a long, ragged breath, struggling to maintain some measure of composure. She'd been in his company for barely five minutes, and already she was ready to forget her own name.

But if she couldn't retain her sanity, at least she could try to hang onto a little dignity, she scolded herself firmly. *Cool and friendly*. It couldn't be that difficult, surely?

CHAPTER SEVEN

THEO allowed himself a small smile of satisfaction as he slid behind the Aston's Alcantara leather steering wheel and clicked the electronic key smoothly into the ignition. The powerful thoroughbred engine purred into life and he eased the sleek car back out of his reserved parking space.

Slowing at the exit to the roundabout, he slanted a glance across at the woman beside him. Also a thoroughbred - that silky honey-gold hair gleaming in the bright sunshine, the haughty tilt of her chin, those long, long legs and dainty feet, with their pale varnished toe-nails peeping out from her raffia mules.

She was wearing a perfume that smelled faintly of tuberose. The scent was beguiling - innocent and wicked at the same time. Like the woman. It was that enigma which was at the root of his obsession with her. And there was only one way to resolve it – although he was beginning to wonder if that would just make it worse.

At the roundabout he took the right turn towards the centre of town. She glanced up at him in surprise. "Where are we going?"

"I'm taking you to visit a building site."

Annis laughed in startled amusement. "Wow. You certainly know how to show a girl a good time!"

"Don't I just?" He slantws her an appreciative glance. The way a woman laughed was always a measure for him of how long he was likely to want to keep her around. Girlish giggles or forced "*Oh-my-gosh-you're-so-funny*" braying were likely to be shown the door in short order. But her laughter was soft, slightly husky, musical. A sound he liked.

Driving across the stone bridge which spanned the river, he turned left at the bottom of the High Street and drew the car to a halt beside the old jam factory.

"Here?" She frowned in some confusion as she peered up at the semi-derelict façade of the building. So – she was either a very good actress, or she really hadn't known what Statham had been planning.

"Here."

They both climbed out of the car and stood looking up at the mess of rusted wire screens, empty window-frames, graffiti-scarred walls. There was even a fair-sized buddleia growing out of a corner of the roof, its straggling branches drooping with heavy racemes of purple flowers.

But beneath the decay, there were still signs of its former art-deco glory – the tall windows separated by fluted columns, the curved corners, the bright-coloured Egyptian-style faience around the wide front door.

He remembered it from when he was a kid, as a thriving business employing several hundred people in the town. But the chill winds of economic change had seen it closed down years ago. Since then it had stood empty and abandoned, an eye-sore and the focus of a creeping neglect which had begun to pervade this whole section of the town.

"You're never thinking of buying this?" Her astonishment seemed genuine.

He smiled a little crookedly, his hands thrust deep in his pockets as he surveyed the broken, weed-strewn tarmac where the lorries used to pull in to be loaded. "I already own it. It was in the Statham portfolio I picked up when I took over the company."

"My *father* owned it?" She stared up in astonishment at the wreck in front of her. "But what on earth would he want with it? Surely he wasn't planning on opening it up again?"

"Quite the contrary. He was planning to knock it down."

"Knock it down?" Her voice rang with indignant protest. "But it's a fabulous old place. Just look at it – those tiles around the door are amazing." She moved closer for a better look, tracing the outline of the stylised lotus-flower pattern. "It's criminal the way it's been let go so badly these past few years."

"I quite agree." Possibly rather more criminal than she was aware, he reflected dryly. "It has a great deal of potential."

She stepped back again to study the whole of the frontage of the building. "So what are *you* going to do with it?"

He had strolled around to open the boot of the car. "Come inside and I'll show you. Here – you'd better put these on."

He had a couple of bright yellow mechanic's boiler-suits in there, and held one of them out to her. She took it from him, a questioning look on her expressive face, and held them up by the shoulders, eyeing them critically.

"You expect me to wear this?"

"If you don't want to get your clothes filthy. You can roll the sleeves up."

She returned him a look of wry amusement. "I'll have to roll everything up!"

But she struggled into it gamely. It really was far too big for her – she had to blouse the top up over the belt, and roll up the cuffs and ankles, but it still looked comical. And rather to his surprise, she was taking it very well, laughing as she held out the baggy legs between her fingers and waddled up and down like Charlie Chaplin.

"And here we have the very last word in elegance for today's stylish workman." Those vivid blue eyes danced merrily. "In this season's colour – Custard Surprise – with interesting dashes of… um… primer? And a few dollops of what looks like engine oil. Made from industrial strength marquee canvas, one size fits all – except when it doesn't!"

He couldn't help but laugh with her. But it was something a lot stronger than simple amusement that hit him like a kick in the solar plexus. When she laughed like that, she was more than gorgeous – she seemed to light up the space around her with a glow that was all her own. He could almost…

But that was a train of thought he didn't wish to pursue. For the past nine years he had lived a one-track life, with women – of whom there had admittedly been a fair few – kept strictly in a separate compartment. He wasn't ready to break down the walls just yet.

And certainly not with George Statham's daughter.

Instead he handed her a yellow hard-hat. "You'd better put this on too," he said, a little more brusquely than he had intended. "I don't have any boots small enough for a woman, but you should be OK - just mind where you step."

Annis felt like a prize idiot. The hard-hat was too big for her, continually tipping down over her eyes, and the coveralls swamped her. But really it was quite funny, she reflected – they looked like a pair of refugees from the chain gang.

Though Theo did fill his out rather well, she couldn't help noticing - even if it was something she'd rather not acknowledge.

He had a key to unlock the graffiti-scrawled metal security door, and she followed him inside, gazing around with interest. Dim light filtered in through the dirty windows, showing her a large semi-circular space which would once have been the imposing entrance to the offices.

The black-and-white terrazzo floor was still in surprisingly good condition, and so were some of the internal doors, with their leaded window-panels. At the back a wide flight of stone stairs, edged with an elaborate wrought iron balustrade, curved up into the shadows above.

"This could be really nice." She stood in the middle of the hall and turned slowly in a circle, gazing around. "It would need cleaning up a bit, of course, and a few repairs."

"The rest of isn't quite so well-preserved," he warned, a note of ironic amusement in his voice. "Through here."

He hadn't exaggerated. To the right was the factory wing, a vast, gloomy hangar-like space with concrete floors puddled with oily water, and peeling walls stained with mould.

There were some marks on the floor where the giant bottling machines had once stood, but there was little else to show for what had once been a busy workplace - a few random bits of metal, a heap of old cardboard files in one corner, a couple of battered wooden benches.

Annis wrinkled her nose. "What on earth are you going to do with this?"

"I've spoken to one of the multi-plex chains about putting in a small two-screen cinema. There's a pretty good customer catchment, with the town itself and the surrounding areas. It looks quite workable."

Her eyes widened in surprise. "That's a brilliant idea! You have to go all the way into York to get to the cinema. It's a real nuisance if you want to… *Durrrgh!*"

A strangled sound escaped her throat as something fluttered high up in the lattice of steel beams above her head. She jumped back in alarm – only to collide with his hard male body, which made her pounding heart race even faster.

Theo laughed, his arm sliding around her waist to steady her. "It's OK – it was just a pigeon."

"Oh…" Suddenly it was difficult to breathe. He was still holding her close, much closer than was necessary to simply help her regain her balance. "It… made me jump."

The glint of mocking amusement in his dark eyes warned her that he wasn't fooled by her excuse. Quite deliberately he let his gaze drift down to her mouth, and then to the ripe shape of her breasts beneath the rough yellow canvas of her boiler-suit.

There was no mistaking what he was thinking – but she felt as if she was trapped in some kind of spell, unable to move…

Unconsciously she had let herself lean into him, so when he abruptly let her go she almost staggered. "Would you like to see the other side of the building?" he suggested blandly.

"Yes – fine." She tried to match his casual tone, though she was all too conscious of the hot pink blush that had risen to her cheeks.

He had been playing with her, just as he had that night after the Mid-Summer Ball, luring her in and then leaving her dangling until she didn't know if she was on her head or her heels. Struggling for some measure of composure, she followed him back across the entrance hall.

The corridor on this side was long and dark, and had the musty smell of damp. Doors on each side opened into a series of gloomy abandoned offices, some still filled with bits of broken furniture – a drunken three-legged desk, a battered metal filing cabinet with two drawers missing.

Theo turned on the tablet computer he had brought from the car, and showed her the architect's drawings on the screen.

"Here we'll have a restaurant, and a few small shops. We're going to gut the inside here, clean up the frontage, pave it and put out some flower tubs. I'm looking for small specialist shops – maybe a bookshop, a florists, that sort of thing."

"I see…" She leaned over to study the image of the front elevation with growing interest. "I like the way you're going to open up the arches into full-length windows – it looks as if it was built that way."

"That's the intention."

"It would certainly bring back some life into the place." She was a little too conscious of how close he was, his shoulder brushing against hers, as if by accident. Very discreetly she edged away from him, careful to keep her breathing under control. "How will you attract businesses to open up here, though? Shops are closing down all along the High Street."

"This is only a part of a bigger scheme. I'll show you the plans for that later. Shall we have a look upstairs?"

"Oh – yes please." At least it would give her the chance to move further away from him, recover herself a little.

They went back to the main entrance, and climbed the curving flight of stairs to the next floor. This was in even more of a mess than downstairs – in places they had to take care where they trod because the floorboards were rotten.

"There'll be three apartments on each of the upper floors. The two outer ones will have two bedrooms each, and the middle one will have just the one. We'll be replacing the wooden floors throughout, and keeping some of the raw brick exposed as feature walls. And all those on this side will have views over the river."

"It sounds very nice." She strolled over to glance out of the window at the view he had promised. "And rather expensive."

"They won't be cheap," he acknowledged. "We'll be marketing them to young professionals - working locally, or possibly in York."

"There are a lot of young people here in town who would want to have their own home. It's not going to be much help to them."

"I agree. That's why I'm planning to develop that patch of land down by the old railway sidings. Two and three-bedroom houses, ideal for first time buyers – and some of them we're building in partnership with a local Housing Association, for rent."

Trumped again, she reflected with a trace of bitter humour. If she wasn't careful she might even find herself beginning to like him – and that could be extremely dangerous. "What about planning permission? Uncle Charles is the chair of the Planning Committee – and he doesn't like you. That could cause problems."

"Then it's fortunate that it's a committee, not a one-man-show. And that's where you come in."

"Oh?"

"I've done my part." He turned off the tablet computer and slid it into the pocket of his boiler-suit. "I've dotted every 'i' and crossed every 't' with the plans - vehicle access, potential noise pollution, aesthetic considerations. Now I need you to work a little of that magical charm on my behalf. A good word in the appropriate ears…"

She turned back to gaze out of the window, though she saw little of the river and the rolling moorland beyond through the mist of tears in her eyes.

Why should she feel hurt that he was making use of her so ruthlessly, exploiting her social connections to get what he wanted? Hadn't he stated from the very start that that was his intention? So then why did he have to try to get her into bed as well? Did he have to have *everything*?

"Don't you think people might think I'm a bit biased, since everyone assumes I'm spending my nights in your bed?"

"You underestimate your standing in this town." There was a note of sardonic humour in his voice. "They're more likely to think that if you're in my bed, maybe I can't be such a bad lot after all."

She shrugged her slim shoulders in a dismissive gesture. "Well, I suppose you can fool some of the people," she quoted with a brittle laugh.

He smiled slowly. "Ah… If your conscience is troubling you about deceiving people into thinking that you're my mistress… We can always remedy that."

He had come up close up behind her, and she stiffened as she felt his hands close around her shoulders, drawing her back against the hard length of his body. He bent his head into the curve of her neck, his mouth finding the sensitive hollow at the base of her throat.

"If they believe you're spending your nights in my bed, I'd be more than happy to prove them right."

She drew in a sharp breath. The sane part of her mind was warning her desperately to resist him - but as his hot tongue swirled over the rapid pulse that beat just beneath her delicate skin she felt her resolve flicker.

And then he let his hands move slowly across her body, tantalisingly slowly, to cup her breasts through the thick yellow cotton boiler-suit. She closed her eyes, her head tipping back against his shoulder, her breath hot and fast on her parted lips.

How could she resist him, when his possessive hands were already claiming the rights that her traitorous body longed to surrender?

Theo felt every quiver as Annis struggled to maintain her defences, felt her melt against him as she was forced to concede the battle. Her breasts were as round and firm as ripe peaches, fitting perfectly into his hands, and even through the coarse thickness of that absurd yellow boiler-suit he could feel the hardening nubs of her nipples beneath his palms.

He hadn't intended this – not here, not now. But she had lured him in, without even seeming to be conscious of what she was doing. It was those eyes – laughing when she forgot her defences, sparking with icy dignity when he had succeeded in goading her, wary as a faun whenever he was a little too close.

How was he supposed to keep his head, when she looked at him like that?

As she melted back against him her spine had curved slightly, lifting her breasts invitingly beneath his caress. She was so exquisitely responsive to his touch – how would she be if he stripped her naked, right now, let his hands wander over every inch of that smooth, creamy skin?

Already her cheeks were slightly flushed, those incredible long silky lashes fluttering against them as if she sensed exactly what he was intending. He wanted her more than any woman he had ever met. Wanted to make love to her…

But even as the thought formed in his brain, he drew back sharply from the word. Love…

No, it wasn't going to be like that. This was supposed to be a business arrangement, spiced with that frisson of mutual sexual attraction. A twenty-first century relationship - two worldly, sophisticated people who both knew the score, and would take their pleasure as it came, without strings.

Until she had decided to up the stakes with that provocative claim that she had never experienced an orgasm.

Maybe she was accustomed to having other men dance on her string, but she would learn that he wasn't so easy to control. Coldly distancing himself from her all-too-beguiling charms, he deliberately moved his hands to the top stud of her boiler-suit, and tugged it apart with one swift snap. He was gratified to hear her sharp intake of breath.

"It wouldn't be every night, of course." His voice was lazily mocking as he moved his hands slowly down to the next stud, already pulled taut across those ripe breasts. He could sense her tension as she waited for what she knew he was going to do next. "A mistress is merely a convenience, not a permanent fixture."

The snap yielded to the rough jerk of his hands, and the remaining fastenings gave way with barely any resistance. "I would expect you to be available whenever it suits me, and to make yourself scarce at other times. Is that clear?"

He felt the movement in her throat as she swallowed hard. So the ice-princess found it a turn-on to be treated like a sex-toy, did she? Interesting…

He pulled the coarse yellow cotton back off her shoulders, trapping her arms against her sides, and with a brusque movement turned her around to face him, swiftly unfastening the tiny pearl buttons down the front of her shirt.

She opened her eyes to stare up at him, but she didn't make a single move to stop him as he pushed her shirt back over she shoulders too, uncovering the ripe creamy swell of her breasts, the dusky peaks of her nipples clearly visible beneath the tight constraint of her delicate lacy bra-cups.

"You'll do whatever I want you to do, you'll make yourself available whenever and wherever I want you," he emphasised ruthlessly. "And in return, you'll make no demands, expect nothing."

The angry flash in her eyes warned him that while her body may be close to surrender, her spirit was still resisting. That was good – the conflict would add a little spice, even though he was quite sure of what the ultimate outcome would be.

Laughing, he slipped his hands beneath her neat little bottom and lifted her off her feet, perching her on the edge of a dusty old cupboard and moving swiftly between her thighs. Her eyes widened in shock as she found herself nestled very intimately against him, and some small sound escaped her soft pink lips – lips he longed to kiss. But not quite yet…

He laid his hands on her warm skin, over her firm, slender midriff. He could feel her ragged breathing, feel the racing beat of her heart. *Oh yes, Miss Statham*, he murmured inside his head. *This time you're going to discover just who's in control.*

He let his fingertips glide slowly upwards, until his thumbs rested just beneath that frivolous lacy scrap of her bra. And to his delight, he found that the clasp was at the front, tucked beneath a tiny lace butterfly. "Now that's what I like," he murmured, softly teasing. "Everything accessible."

With a deft movement he unfastened the hook, and drew the lace aside. Her skin had a soft sheen like creamy silk; freed from their constraint, her naked breasts were as round and firm as ripe peaches, tipped with tautly puckered nipples of a delicate shade of pink. He let his gaze linger there for a long, long moment, savouring the prospect of finding out just how responsive those pert little buds could be.

"Beautiful…"

Annis held her breath as she felt the heat of his eyes roaming over her fevered skin, burning as if he was branding her. How could she let him do this to her? But she was helpless to stop him – she knew that in some treacherous part of her mind she wanted it to happen.

His smile taunted her, making her wait, knowing exactly what the anticipation was doing to her. And then very slowly he stroked his hands up over the smooth curve of her stomach to cup her breasts in his palms, the pad of his thumbs rolling across each taut, tender nipple.

She let go her breath in a shuddering little moan of pleasure. She felt as if her insides were melting, every feminine part of her responding to his exquisite touch.

He laughed, huskily soft. "So much for the ice-princess. I told you I would know how to set your body on fire. '*Wherever and whenever I want you.*' And you're going to enjoy every minute of it."

To her shame, she was forced to admit that it was true. She had no way to resist him. His hands were caressing both breasts, his sensitive, clever fingers teasing and tormenting, tracing lazy, tantalising circles around the taut pink peaks, lightly pinching at the sweetly sensitised buds until they felt as if they had been touched by a flame.

And as his head bent over hers, his hot mouth roving over her trembling eyelids and down to the delicate shell of her ear, his hard teeth nibbling sensuously at her lobe, she shivered with heat, all her defences crumbling to dust.

His hungry mouth moved on into the hollow of her shoulder, his hot tongue finding again that racing pulse at the base of her throat, and then on down...

Her head tipped back, her spine a quivering arc, lifting her aching breasts invitingly towards him and closing the angle between their bodies even further so that heat pooled in her stomach as she felt the hard jut of his maleness nudging against her most intimate feminine core.

His head bent over the ripe naked swell, his sinuous tongue lapping and swirling around the taut pink peaks, and she heard herself moaning softly as his mouth closed at last over one ripe bud, nipping at it lightly with his hard teeth, swirling it with his moist, rasping tongue, suckling on it with a deep, tugging rhythm that sent a fever racing through her veins.

It was the most exquisite torture. Images were swirling in her head, flagrantly erotic images of him stripping off the rest of her clothes, laying her back across the rickety cupboard and making hot, hard love to her right here among all the dust and debris of the semi-derelict building.

And as his mouth finally moved to claim hers, and his tongue plundered deep into the sweet, defenceless valley of her mouth, it seemed as though he too had been caught up in the same wild surge of desire.

She knew she would regret it – tonight, tomorrow... He was offering her nothing more than a fleeting moment of physical pleasure – he had made it more than clear that he wasn't interested in anything more. That cold heart probably wasn't capable of love. But if this was all she could have, she would settle for it willingly.

And he knew it. "I could have you right now, couldn't I?" His voice was velvet against her ear.

A small quiver ran through her. He was deliberately humiliating her, forcing her to acknowledge her own defeat.

"Admit it," he persisted. "I could take you on the floor of this dump, and you'd do whatever I wanted you to, wouldn't you?"

"Yes." It was no more than a ragged whisper.

His laughter was chilling. "It's a tempting thought," he conceded, letting his eyes rake down over her flushed, half-naked body. "But I prefer to be a little more comfortable. Besides, it's time for lunch. Don't forget to mind where you tread," he added as he strolled towards the door. "You don't want to put your foot through the floorboards."

She stared after him, shaking in shock, her cheeks a hot scarlet. Yet again he had quite calculatedly taken her to the brink of total surrender – and then he had just walked away! Put her foot through the floorboards? She'd like to put it through his head!

Her fingers felt like thumbs as she hastily fumbled to fasten the clip of her bra and pull her clothing up over her shoulders. Still doing up the buttons, she marched after him – the effect slightly marred by having to skip smartly around one of those places he had warned her about, where the floorboards were rotten and dangerous.

He was waiting for her by the front door, key in hand. She stalked past him, her nose in the air. "I'm afraid you're going to have eat lunch on your own," she announced frostily. "I'm going home."

"You mean the deal's off?" The hard note in his voice warned her that there were only two options – do exactly as he wanted, or lose everything.

"You broke the terms." She was struggling to keep her voice steady.

"No I didn't. I promised I wouldn't resort to financial coercion to get you into bed. I didn't notice much coercion going on back there – financial or otherwise. In fact you seemed to be more than willing to participate."

He flicked the central locking as he strolled over to the car, opening the boot and tossing in his hard-hat. Then he began to peel off his yellow boiler-suit.

Annis hesitated, her mouth dry, as she watched, mesmerised by every lithe movement – the easy shrug of his wide shoulders as he pulled his arms out of the rough canvas, the athletic grace as he stepped out of the legs.

He tossed the suit into the boot, then glanced at her, one dark eyebrow arched in question as he waited for her to make up her mind what she was going to do.

She knew that she should walk away. That would be the sensible thing to do, the safe thing. But sensible had very little to do with it – and nor, if she was completely honest, did the money.

In fact it would almost be better if he *was* using financial coercion to get her into bed – at least then she could pretend to herself that she didn't really have a choice.

No – what was luring her in was far stronger than that. It was something inside of her, far beyond the reach of reason, some purely instinctive response as old as Eve – the response of a woman to a powerful male.

She could feel a blush of pink rise to her cheeks as she began to unsnap the studs down the front of her own boiler-suit, remembering all too vividly how he had unsnapped them just a short time ago. Struggling for some kind of composure, she half-turned away from him while she stripped off the inelegant outfit, and handed it to him with her arm extended at full length.

He took it from her with a faintly mocking smile, dropped it on top of everything else and closed the boot, then walked to the passenger door, holding it open for her.

He didn't speak – if he had said a word she would have turned on her heel and walked away. Instead she contented herself with tilting up her chin, sliding past him to keep as far away from him as possible as she settled herself into the passenger seat.

He closed the door and came round to swing in beside her, the knowing glint in those dark eyes making speech unnecessary. He knew, without having to make the point. She was caught in his spell, and there wasn't a thing she could do about it.

CHAPTER EIGHT

ANNIS gave Theo the silent treatment all the way to the restaurant, staring out of the window at the passing scenery – not that it seemed to bother him in the slightest. He had flicked on the in-car stereo, filling the car with the sound of Aretha Franklin belting out some hot soul. She had to concentrate to stop herself tapping her fingers along with the rhythm.

She might have known he would have booked a table at the most exclusive hotel in the district, she reflected wryly as he swung into the car park of the White Swan. The Aston Martin looked quite at home among the ranks of Porches, Mercedes and Jaguars. And of course, once again they would be seen together, reinforcing the gossip.

"Show time," she hissed as she unfastened her seat belt and climbed out of the car. He arched one eyebrow in cynical amusement, letting one hand rest possessively on the small of her back as he steered her towards the elegant entrance.

Everything gleamed – gilt-framed mirrors, mahogany panelling, marble floors. She had been here before, of course, numerous times, but she was a little surprised when the doorman greeted Theo by name, and the head waiter himself hurried out to show them to the best table, in the corner of the wide terrace which overlooked the curve of the river.

She couldn't help but be aware of the way almost every woman in the place watched Theo as they made their way between the tables. She wasn't surprised. There was something so compellingly male about him – those wide shoulders beneath his crisp white shirt, the easy athleticism in the way he moved.

As they reached their table, he drew out her chair for her. She took it with a murmured, "Thank you" - she wasn't going to let him make her forget her manners. But when the head waiter offered her a menu, she took it with a much firmer, "Thank you," and her most dazzling smile.

She glanced quickly over the selection, and chose an iced cucumber soup, followed by a peppered salmon with a mozzarella salad. "I'll have the same." Theo didn't even glance at the menu. "And a sparkling mineral water."

"The same for me," Annis added.

Sitting across the table from him, Annis was finding it difficult to keep her heartbeat steady. Resting her arm on the wooden balustrade beside her, she turned her gaze out over the river, where swans sailed majestically along the reeded banks, and herons fished in the shade of the graceful willows which dipped their branches into the tranquil water flowing by.

Not far from where they sat, a vivid blue kingfisher was perched on a low branch, intently watching the water below, waiting for a fish. So patient... And then with a sudden flash it swooped down, and in a split second was back on its perch, a sliver of silver caught in its beak.

Theo laughed softly. "If I'd known you were so interested in bird-watching I'd have brought you a pair of binoculars."

She returned him a look of cool disdain. "I don't have anything to say to you."

He arched one quizzical eyebrow. "No? You all but let me make love to you, and ten minutes later you can't even hold a conversation with me?"

"That wasn't making love. That was..."

"What?" He supplied a very Anglo-Saxon alternative, but somehow the huskiness of his voice, and the dark gleam in his eyes, lent it a potent eroticism it never had when scrawled on toilet walls.

Annis felt her cheeks flame scarlet, her eyes darting around to make sure no-one could hear them.

Theo laughed softly. "Whatever you choose to call it, it's going to be good. We both know that."

She picked up her fork and began doodling with the point on the white damask tablecloth. "It isn't going to happen. I told you..."

"I know what you told me. But after what happened back there, you can hardly expect me to believe you, can you?"

"I don't care what you believe..."

Her heated protest was interrupted by the arrival of the waiter with their soup, followed by the head waiter once again to ensure that everything was exactly as it should be, that the soup was chilled to the right temperature and that it was neither too sweet nor too salty.

By the time he had gone, Annis was able to recover a little of her composure.

"You certainly get the best service." She injected a deliberate note of sardonic humour into her voice as she watched the man's retreating back, weaving nimbly between the tables, noting every detail as he passed. "The personal attention of the head waiter, no less. I always thought he was rather grand."

"Not too grand to attend to every customer's needs, I hope. But he may be a little more attentive to me – I own the place."

She stared at him in startled amazement. "It was *you* who bought it? Dad was absolutely furious, but he couldn't find out who had bid against him."

Theo smiled, though his eyes were hard. "I didn't like his plans for modernising it. I've always been rather fond of it. My mother used to work here when I was a kid, in the kitchens – sometimes I used to come over and play in the gardens. Before she died."

Annis felt her breath catch in her throat. She'd never heard him mention his mother before – she just knew she'd died when he was… it would probably have been when he was about ten years old. But she sensed that the last thing he wanted was sympathy.

"I'm… rather glad you did out-bid him, to be honest," she conceded reluctantly. "Unfortunately, when it comes to modernisation, Dad really didn't have the best of taste."

"Well, if the décor of his office was anything to go by…"

That reminder set Annis on edge again. "Well, now you own the place you can do whatever you like with it."

"True."

She laughed without humour. "You went to a lot of effort to get it - you must be very pleased with yourself. Do you always get what you want?"

"When I want it enough."

His dark eyes glittered with sinful promise, and she felt

her cheeks grow hot. He didn't need to put the implication into words. Studying him from beneath her lashes, she was forced to admit that he was also a man whom a woman could very easily fall in love with.

It wasn't just his looks, or his intelligence, or that air of cool self-assurance. There was something to admire in the fact that he had pulled himself up by his own bootstraps, parlaying his engineering expertise into the foundation of a very successful business empire.

And then there was that uncompromising maleness, which touched a core of pure feminine response, far beyond the reach of reason.

But it would be bad enough to succumb to the almost irresistible temptation to sleep with him, she reminded herself warily - it would be just plain crazy to fall in love with him.

The waiter had come to take their empty soup bowls and serve them with their peppered salmon. For a while Annis concentrated on the food, a sensual experience in itself. The salmon was soft and flaky, melting on her tongue, the peppers giving it a piquancy that lingered between bites.

But it wasn't just the hot pepper sauce which was igniting a fever in her blood. The memory of the way Theo Lander had touched her seemed to be seared onto her skin as if he had branded her.

As the waiter replaced their plates with coffee, she was beginning to find the silence stretching between them rather uncomfortable. "You… um… said the Jam Factory was part of a bigger scheme," she reminded him, searching a little desperately for a neutral topic of conversation. "What do you have in mind?"

Theo smiled, recognising that that veneer of composure was wafer-thin. It was seriously tempting to goad her that little bit further – that blaze of temper that erupted when he provoked her was a glorious sight. But regrettably he had other priorities at the moment.

He took the tablet computer from the slim briefcase at his feet, and laid it on the table so they could both see the screen. The page he opened showed a detailed map of the area around the High Street.

"The starting point will be this block here, between Lord Street and Jervis Street." As he touched the screen several of the buildings outlined transformed into a translucent blue. "The buildings are basically sound, they just need some refurbishment to make them let-able."

He touched the screen again, and a street-view image rose from the map, showing an artist's impression of new shop-fronts.

"Realistically, retail shops are going to be less and less of a feature in the future – they're losing out to the internet and out-of-town retail parks. But I don't want all solicitors' offices and charity shops. I'll be looking for a good mix, the kind of businesses that can't be replaced on-line."

"Like hairdressers?" she suggested.

"Exactly." He smiled across the table at her – he had known she would be quick to grasp the concept. "Then I'm thinking perhaps a doctor's surgery, a pre-school nursery... This site here, where Woolworth's used to be, would be an ideal size for a fitness centre."

"That'll be popular."

"And I'll be making sure there are several cafés for people to stop and sit down, and good car-parking facilities." More taps on the key brought images of more shops, then another area behind them marked in orange. "There, where the old Elim Chapel used to be, before they pulled it down - we'll be putting a three-storey car-park there. Access will be almost directly from the by-pass without even having to drive into the town."

She was studying the map with interest, running her fingers over the touch-screen features to make the various elevations pop up one after the other. "You're going to buy up all these buildings?"

He shook his head. "They were part of the Statham portfolio which your father mortgaged – the main part of the company's assets."

She glanced up at him, a look of confusion shadowing those violet eyes. "My father owned them? But… So why didn't he do something with them, instead of just letting them sit there and rot?"

"He wasn't interested in doing anything with them." Across the table he was studying her reaction. Had she really known nothing of her father's intentions? He was beginning to think so. "He had… other plans."

"Oh?" There was a hint of uncertainty in her voice. She wasn't going to like what she was about to hear.

"He was going to demolish most of the High Street," Theo told her bluntly. "And build a casino and nightclub complex, with a hotel on the jam factory site."

"A *casino*?" She stared at him, plainly shocked. "How do you know that?"

"I found all the plans when I took over the company. He'd been working on it for a long time, buying up the premises, putting up the rents so that the shops couldn't survive. He knew there'd be opposition to his plans in the town, so he aimed to let the whole High Street run down, until eventually people would accept anything rather than let it stand derelict."

"But…" Annis hesitated, her protest fading on her lips. It sounded all too plausible. Her mind went back over the past few years, remembering passing comments that had seemed meaningless at the time, which now suddenly made a very unwelcome sense. But it was still difficult to take it in. "He'd still have had to get the permission of the planning committee."

"And as you pointed out to me earlier, who is the Chair of the planning committee?"

"Uncle Charles…" She shook her head in disbelief. "Are you saying they had some sort of conspiracy going?"

"I don't have any proof. But it wouldn't be the first time."

Annis felt a cold chill creeping down her spine. "You're talking about when my father bought your land. I know he took advantage of you, and then made a nice profit on it. But if you thought he was cheating you, you could have sold it to someone else."

"Not when no-one could get planning permission to even build an extension to the house."

"You think my father conspired with Uncle Charles?"

"You don't think it seems rather a coincidence, that within three months of your father buying the land, the position of the planning committee was completely reversed?"

"So that's why you set out to ruin him." Something twisted in the pit of her stomach. "You couldn't rest until you had your revenge."

"I set out to ruin him," he acknowledged, his voice as hard as steel. "But not just because of the land. He ruined my father. He spent two years in prison for a crime he didn't commit. He was a strong man, but it broke him – physically and mentally. He died six months after he came out."

"You can't claim my father was responsible for that."

"I can't prove it in a court of law. But I know it was him, as sure as I'm sitting here." There was a whiteness around his mouth, betraying his tension. "He had been trying to buy our land for more than a year, but my father refused to sell. He'd taken my mother home to that house as a bride, and it was full of memories of her. He would never have parted with it."

His hand curled into a fist.

"The last time Statham called, trying to browbeat my father with threats, I threw him out of the house. He stood at the gate and warned us we'd regret getting in his way. My father just laughed - he didn't believe Statham could do anything to hurt him." He laughed himself, a harsh, angry sound. "He had no idea how wrong he was."

Annis said nothing. Unconsciously she reached for a sachet of sugar, twisting it in her fingers.

"It was a few weeks later that the re-spray job came in." Theo's voice was flat. "Dad thought it was a little odd at the time – the car was less than two years old, and there was absolutely nothing wrong with it. But the woman who brought it in – of course there was a woman involved – insisted she'd changed her mind about the colour."

His mouth was a grim line. "She said she'd been quoted some ridiculous amount to do the work by a garage in York, but then someone had recommended her to come to Tom Lander. Needless to say it turned out that no garage in York had ever heard of her, and the person who was supposed to have recommended her was never identified."

He laughed bitterly. "She wound poor Dad around her little finger - he was always an easy touch for a pretty woman. She made a big fuss about security – said she didn't want her precious car to get stolen. He promised her it would be quite safe in the lock-up, and she batted her eyelashes at him as she handed over the keys. We never saw her again."

He paused, his dark eyes shadowed with anger – and pain. "Two days later the police arrived with a search warrant. They were acting on a tip-off that Dad was involved in a stolen car racket, they said. He was supposed to be re-spraying cars to order so that they could be sold on as legitimate to some unsuspecting buyer. And there was the evidence, right there in the lock-up, the primer still damp on the panels."

"But… If that's what happened, why did your father plead guilty?" Annis protested, bewildered.

"He got a warning – a phone call, the week before he went to court. He was told in no uncertain terms that if he didn't plead guilty, I'd be dragged into it too." His mouth twisted into a crooked smile. "He didn't tell me that until a few months later."

He drew in a deep breath before continuing, clearly finding the story difficult to relate. "The prosecution offered him a deal. If he would name his 'associates' he would get off with a lighter sentence. But he couldn't name anyone – he didn't have any associates. So he got three years. We had to sell the house to pay the legal fees. And there was only one person to sell it to." His hand had clenched into a fist. "No, I could never prove he was behind it. But I knew."

Annis didn't quite know what to say. If this was true… "You… couldn't find the woman?"

He shook his head. "She'd given a false name and address, of course. To be honest, I don't think the police were ever really serious about looking for her. They believed they had their man – why bother? Especially when they're short of manpower."

"Couldn't you have tried a private detective?"

He smiled dryly. "You've been reading too many lurid novels. As a matter of fact we did try it, but it's pretty expensive – we could only afford to hire one for a few days. Unfortunately Dad couldn't give a very clear description of her. Blonde, maybe around forty but well preserved. Looked the sort who could afford to indulge a whim over the colour of her car."

"She doesn't sound like the sort of woman who would get involved in something like that," Annis mused.

"You don't believe me." He sounded more resigned than annoyed.

"I'm sure you believe it," she responded carefully. "But if I have to choose between believing your father and believing mine, can you blame me for picking mine?"

"I suppose not." He acknowledged the point with a slight shrug of his shoulders. "Another coffee?"

"No thank you."

He caught the eye of one of the young waiters, signalling to him to bring the bill, which he simply signed with a fluid scrawl.

"I'm going to be away for the next ten days," he said. "The Jam Factory comes before the planning committee next month. I want you to arrange a dinner party for the Friday after I return, and invite anyone you think may be helpful."

"You rate my influence very highly." She tried to inject a lilt of amusement into her voice.

"Yes I do." Across the table his eyes captured hers in a dark, level gaze. "I don't believe I'm mistaken."

"Well, I'll… do what I can. But not for you. I'll do it because I like the plans you've shown me. I think they'll be good for the town."

"That's all you need to say "

♥ ♥ ♥

"So how's it going?"

122

"Excellent." Annis stroked her hand gently down the trembling flank of the bay mare, the latest resident of the stables. She had intended to make it clear to the Horse Rescue Society that she couldn't take any more, but there was no way she could have turned this one away. "I have two more horses coming next week for schooling, and another three enquiries in the pipeline."

Vicky chuckled with laughter, adjusting herself to a better position under the mare's swollen abdomen. "I didn't mean that. I meant with Theo."

"Oh, that." Annis lifted her slender shoulders in a shrug meant to convey casual indifference. "It's going OK."

"You're still seeing him?"

"On and off." She hadn't even told Vicky the truth about their 'arrangement.' Maybe it would have been easier if she had – keeping up the pretence with her best friend was one of the most difficult parts of the whole damned thing.

"Oh, Miss Butter-Wouldn't-Melt-in-your-Mouth." Vicky's eyes danced. "You can't fool me. I saw the way you were looking at each other the night of the Midsummer Ball. Talk about giving off sparks - I thought you were going to set the whole place on fire!"

Annis laughed a little edgily. "You're imagining things."

It was three days since the… incident in the jam factory. Although she hadn't seen Theo since he had dropped her back at her car after their lunch at the White Swan, she was still struggling to put what had happened out of her mind.

It wasn't easy. The summer nights were hot, and she had lain awake till the early hours, remembering the way those dark eyes had looked at her, the way his hands had caressed her naked breasts…

"Anyway, how's this lady?" Bending to peer at her friend, she dismissed all thoughts of Theo Lander from her head. "Certainly not imagining things, I would think?"

"No, she's in foal all right." Vicky straightened and began to pack the portable ultrasound back into its case. "Quite well gone, too, I'd guess. It's hard to tell exactly – she's in such poor condition, the foal could be small for the gestation period.

You'll need to keep an eye on her – don't hesitate to call me out if it looks like trouble. She might need help – possibly even a Caesarean."

"Oh dear – I hope it won't come to that." The nervous mare was still wary, but she did allow her nose to be stroked.

"Do you have a name for her?"

"I thought I'd call her Amber."

"That's nice," Vicky approved as they let themselves out of the stable, bolting it carefully behind them.

The stable yard was a hive of activity. It was the first week of the school holidays, and nearly all the young volunteer helpers had come in to give the place a thorough clean-up. The yard was looking very smart, with all the stables hosed out and disinfected, their doors freshly varnished and all the hinges oiled.

"Thanks for coming out."

"No problem."

"Coffee?"

"I won't say no," Vicky agreed readily as they strolled up through the stable-yard towards the back door of the house. "By the way, is it true that Theo's bought up the old jam factory on Emstry Road? It's about time something was done about that old place – it's been an eyesore ever since it closed down."

"Yes, he has." Dammit, why did her friend have to keep harping on about that damned man? "He's planning to do it up, put in some shops on the ground floor, and apartments upstairs. He's even looking at opening a cinema – you know, one of those little Multi-Plex places."

"That's brilliant - just what the town needs. I was saying to Gordon only the other day, I can't remember the last time I went to the cinema. It's such a hassle, having to go all the way into York just to catch a film."

Vicky was still chattering merrily about her favourite movies as they walked through the scullery into the hall. But Annis stopped dead in the doorway, her heart sinking. Joan was at the front door, and beyond her shoulder she could see the florist's van.

Damn...

The housekeeper turned with a huge bunch of yellow roses in her arms. "*Another* bunch." Her voice was vibrant with excitement. "That's every day for over a week now. No card again," she added archly.

Vicky laughed in delight. "Well, I wonder who on earth they could be from? Um... let me think. Who could be sending you roses?"

"You know perfectly well who they're from." To her annoyance, Annis could feel her cheeks flush a hot pink.

"So he's sending you roses. It must be love! I'd better go home and dig out my wedding hat."

"You won't be needing it. It's just... very casual. No big deal."

"Oh, come on. A man doesn't send a woman roses every day unless he's really keen. I told you... Oh bugg..." Her cellphone had warbled in her pocket. "Looks like I won't have time for that coffee after all. Duty calls!"

Annis waved her friend off, then closed the door and turned back to the hall table, where Joan had left the roses. She stood looking down at them, touching her fingertip to one velvet petal. Already their heady perfume was mingling with the beeswax from Joan's busy morning polishing.

Roses and wedding hats...

Joan came bustling through from the kitchen, triumphantly bearing a tall glass vase. "This ought to do. We're beginning to run out of vases - I had to root right in the back of the cupboard to find this one! But they've got nice long stems so they should be OK. Shall I put them in the lounge, with the others?"

Annis conceded defeat with a small sigh. "Yes please."

She couldn't help but wonder how enthusiastic Joan would have been about the roses if she knew how close she had come to losing her job because of Theo Lander's machinations.

She had agonised over the extravagance of employing the housekeeper for days, but she had worked here for more than forty years, since Annis's mother was a little girl. She had vowed to keep her on for as long as she possibly could.

Joan selected a couple of the finest blooms to form the centre-piece of the display and tucked them into place. "He's done pretty well for himself, Tom Lander's lad. Betty Dillon in the Post Office was telling me the other day that there was a bit about him in one of them magazines – you know, the ones with all the gossip in, about all the telly stars and footballer's wives? I don't read that stuff myself, of course," she added, assuming an air of dignity. "Anyway, it had a list of the top one hundred most eligible bachelors in the country, and young Theo was on the list. A tycoon, they called him."

"Good for him," Annis murmured, wishing that for just five minutes she could get away from the subject of Theo Lander.

"You could do a lot worse for yourself." Joan smiled, a romantic gleam in her eyes. "He was always such a nice boy. Always so polite and honest - like his dad."

"Like his dad?" Annis was startled by the housekeeper's words - there had been something quite decisive about them, as if they had been chosen with some deliberation.

The older woman nodded. "Tom Lander was a good man. There wasn't no-one as knew him believed he did what he was sent to prison for. He never did a dishonest thing in his life. Why, he wouldn't even have kept a pound coin he found lying in the street."

Annis turned to stare at her. "Even though he pleaded guilty?"

"Aye, so he did," the older woman conceded, her plain face set in obstinate lines. "But that still don't mean he did it."

♥

Annis sat in the big leather chair in her father's study, staring at his desk. Most of the drawers were empty now – Theo's lawyer had spent a couple of days going through them, taking all the important papers, and she had thrown away the rest. She rested her elbows on the old-fashioned blotter, and dropped her chin into her hands.

Joan's words were still running through her head, and the story Theo had told her. She had said she preferred to believe her own father, but that wasn't strictly true. She knew how ruthless her father could be when it came to making money. Just how far would he have gone?

The key to it was the woman who was supposed to have brought the car in. Blonde… Her father had always had a taste for blondes, she remembered wryly. Even while her mother had been alive, there had been blondes…

Suddenly she sat up straight. Of course it was a long time ago, but maybe there was something… Her eyes flickered around the room. If the woman had been one of his mistresses, would he have kept some kind of memento of her?

He had never been the sentimental sort, but he *had* been possessive of his acquisitions – and he had always regarded his women as falling into that category. So maybe he had kept some kind of trophy?

She had found nothing in the desk, but… She got up and walked across to the bookcase, running her fingers along the edges of the shelves. She didn't really know what she was looking for. She tried to cast her mind back in time.

On the rare occasions when he had been at home, he always used to spend most of his time in here. And yet with all these books, she rarely saw him reading one – they'd mostly belonged to her grandfather. There was a full set of Dickens, bound in dark red leather, the plays of Oscar Wilde…

She spotted it eventually, up on the top shelf – a brown envelope tucked in between a couple of hard-back volumes of Wisden from the 1950s. Kicking a leather pouffé into place with her foot, she stood on it and reached up to pull the envelope down. Carrying it over to the desk, she spilled the contents across the blotter.

Photographs. Taken over a number of years, to judge from her father's changing appearance in different photos – the hairline progressively receding, the waistline expanding.

Most of them seemed to have been taken in bars and nightclubs, in various exotic locations - no doubt when he'd been on one of his many 'business' trips abroad. And in every one, he had his arm slung casually around the shoulders of a different woman – most of them blondes.

Sifting through, she picked out a couple which looked as if they had been taken around nine years ago, and studied them more carefully.

One in particular caught her eye. She had bought that orange spotted tie for him for his fiftieth birthday. Nine years ago. The woman draped around him was slim and attractive, her hair stylishly highlighted, her red dress expensive. And her face was vaguely familiar…

Mining deep into the recesses of her memory, she found the clue. Uncle Charles's secretary, from his main office in York. Her name was Carol, or Claire – something like that.

Her eye fell on her father's leather-bound address book. She pulled it towards her and flicked it open, turning the pages one by one, scanning her father's scrawling script. And there it was – Caroline Thompson. She was sure that was her. If she remembered rightly, she had moved to London with her husband around the time Tom Lander was arrested.

The address in the book was for her old address in York – there was no address for London. Uncle Charles may know it - but would he give it to her? If his secretary had been involved in the conspiracy, it was possible that he had been involved too.

There was one person she knew who could find out. Sandy was a journalist on the local paper. If there was any truth in Theo's story, Sandy would dig it out. For a moment she hesitated. Maybe she should wait and speak to Theo about it first. But it might all come to nothing.

Besides, it was her father – it was her responsibility. Drawing in a deep breath, she reached out and picked up the telephone.

CHAPTER NINE

"PLANNING CHIEF QUITS IN CONSPIRACY SCANDAL."

The local paper was tucked into the top of Joan's shopping basket. Annis hadn't read the article yet – she really wasn't sure she wanted to. She knew she had been right to do what she had done, but she still felt like a traitor. Her own father, and Uncle Charles…

"Well, it's a good thing it's all finally come out." Joan was wielding a bread knife vigorously over a home-baked ciabatta. "I knew old Tom Lander was innocent. It's just a shame he isn't here to see it. But I'll bet young Theo is pleased. What did he say?"

"I don't know – I haven't spoken to him." Very carefully Annis spooned the pistachio and vanilla parfait mix into the chocolate baskets lined up on the baking tray. "He's… been abroad. The Far East somewhere."

Adding the finishing flourish – a pistachio nut and a vanilla pod on each individual basket – she carefully carried the tray over to the fridge. "Well, that's done – I just have time to get ready now, before anyone gets here. Thanks for coming over to help, Joan." She slid her arm around the housekeeper's plump shoulders and gave them a squeeze. "I would never have got it all done without you."

"No problem," the housekeeper assured her comfortably. "I love cooking up these grand dishes, and I don't get the chance very often. My Don just likes good plain cooking – he won't eat nothing fancy."

Annis laughed, and slipped away before Joan could return to her favourite subject – Theo Lander, and why he was still sending roses every day. Annis suspected it was because he had forgotten to tell his secretary to cancel the order.

Before going upstairs to change, she popped in quickly to check the dining room. The table looked beautiful – her mother's best linen tablecloth, rarely used over the past few years, was set with the finest crystal glassware and silver cutlery. Bowls of roses – yellow roses – made a glowing centrepiece, set off with delicate sprigs of fern from the garden.

Crossing the room, she pushed open the wide French doors which led onto the terrace, to try to bring a breath of air into the room, but there wasn't even a whisper of breeze.

The past week had been *hot* – day after day with the temperature soaring well into the nineties. The papers had been full of pictures of baking bodies in bikinis on every beach around the coast, and the nights were so humid it had been difficult to sleep.

It had been hard work in the stables, making sure that all the horses had plenty to drink, checking if any of them were getting over-heated, sponging them down with cool water if necessary.

And on top of all that, she was throwing a dinner party for a dozen people, at Theo Lander's behest.

With a small sigh she crossed the hall and climbed the stairs. Her head was aching slightly – though whether it was just the heat, or the thought of seeing Theo again after two longs weeks she wasn't sure.

Two weeks since he had kissed her in the derelict jam factory – two weeks when she hadn't been able to get that kiss out of her mind.

But tonight she really needed to maintain her composure. That newspaper article had shifted the ground between them, and she had no idea what the impact of that shift would be, how Theo would react.

Plus everyone would be watching her, wondering about her reaction to the scandal. No-one knew she had been the source of the story, not even Vicky – she had asked Sandy to keep her role secret. Though she suspected that Theo would guess.

She had already showered, but she gave her hands and throat another splash of cold water to try to combat the sultry heat of the evening. Sitting down at her dressing table, she chose just the minimum of make-up – any more would simply melt away. A skim of tinted moisturizer, a flick of navy-blue mascara on her lashes, and the merest hint of coral lip-gloss to match her carefully-manicured nails.

She had been planning to put her hair up, but in the end it seemed like too much bother. Instead she brushed it back from one side of her face, catching it up with a couple of tortoiseshell combs, and let it fall in a curling wave over the other shoulder.

A quick spritz of her favourite tuberose perfume, and she was ready to step into her dress – the slim black sheath she had originally planned to wear to the Mid-Summer Ball. Slipping her feet into her high-heeled black sandals, she drew in a long, deep breath and walked from the room.

♥

The dinner party was going well. Theo felt a certain satisfaction – he had known that Annis would have talent for this sort of thing. The menu was perfect for such a hot evening – the fillet of salmon in a wild mushroom sauce had been delicious, and the subtle flavours of the creamy desert had tempted him to abandon his usual custom of refusing a sweet and skipping straight to the coffee.

But a dinner party depended on much more than food, he mused, glancing around the table. She had chosen a good mix of guests, all of them meeting his primary criteria – that they should be people who could influence opinion in the town.

And she had kept a lively conversation going. He watched her covertly as she responded to what someone was saying with a ripple of that musical laughter, her eyes dancing merrily.

A familiar tightening caught him in the gut. Dammit, he wanted her.

He had recognised the danger from the beginning, and had tried to deal with it by focussing on the purely carnal aspects of his attraction. But it hadn't worked. Physically he wanted her more than ever – it gnawed at him, distracting him from whatever else he tried to concentrate on.

But it wasn't just the physical thing – it was something far more complex than that. He wanted to share her laughter, wanted to watch her wake up in the mornings, wanted to see her across a crowded room and know that she would be going home with him.

Dammit, it wasn't supposed to have been like this. Women had a place in his life, but it had always been a place defined by specific boundaries. For the past nine years he had been too focussed on achieving his ambition to take the time for a relationship.

And he wasn't sure that he was ready yet for the complications a relationship could bring. Particularly with George Statham's daughter…

George Statham.

The irony of it was really quite amusing, he reflected dryly. Without George Statham, he might still have been comfortably working in his father's garage. It had been his own fierce desire for pay-back that had spurred him to achieve the success he had. So in a way, he had Statham to thank for where he was today.

And now, at last, the truth had come out – the proof that his father was innocent, that George Statham was guilty.

How did Annis feel about it? He hadn't had a chance to speak to her in private yet. His business in Singapore had taken longer than he had planned, and then his flight had been delayed by bad weather, and by the time he had arrived tonight most of the other guests had already been here.

He was pretty sure that she was the source of the story – who else could it have been? So why had she done it – knowing that it was likely to lead to a massive scandal and destroy her father's reputation?

Watching her across the table, he knew the answer to that. Because it was the right thing to do. Her charm wasn't just a superficial gloss – it was a bone-deep part of her.

How wrong he had been about her! He had treated her badly, and she really hadn't deserved it. But tonight he would make it up to her.

And then…?

That newspaper article had been a game changer. He hadn't worked out the new rules yet.

Annis stirred a swirl of cream into her coffee. The evening had been quite a strain. From the moment he had arrived, she had been constantly aware of Theo, as if there was some kind of invisible force-field between them.

She was conscious of him now, those dark eyes watching her across the table, and she could feel the knot of tension in the pit of her stomach tighten. It was real a struggle to maintain her composure.

People had been skirting politely around the news of the week - but it was inevitable that as the wine flowed and everyone began to relax, someone would bring it up. It was Jeremy, clumsily expressing sympathy for the shock she must have had on finding out the news, who drew her laughing disclaimer.

"Oh no – I'm afraid nothing my father did would ever have shocked me." She infused a not of light amusement into her voice. "Does that show a lack of filial piety? I just wish it had all come out at the time – it would have saved other people a good deal of pain."

"Yes, of course." Vicky turned to Theo, her eyes bright with empathy. "It must have come as big relief to you, Theo."

He smiled back. "Indeed. Like Annis, I would have preferred it to have come out a long time ago, but better late than never."

"You know, I always suspected old Charles was on the take." It was Gerald Trenchard who had spoken – Annis couldn't help reflecting acidly that he had shown no sign of any such reservations before the rose fertiliser had struck the air-conditioning system. "Planning in this town has been a mess for years."

"But now we have a chance to get it right," Vicky's husband pointed out. "It's a brilliant opportunity – it could bring the town to life again."

"Well, I for one am in favour of more shops" Sara Forsyth raised her glass as if toasting the prospect in champagne.

"So long as one of them's a shoe shop!" That provoked general laughter around the table.

"What we could do with is some new housing. Something young families can afford."

"You're planning to build houses on that land down by the old shunting yard, aren't you Theo?" Annis put in, subtly guiding the discussion as he had wanted her to.

"That's right." His eyes signalled his appreciation of her tactics. "Pete, why don't you tell them about it?"

"Oh… Yes, of course. Well, you see, the aim is develop affordable homes. Of course one of the biggest cost factors in housing development is land prices, so of course the fact that it's a brown-field site will be a big help…"

Theo sat back in his seat, watching the effect. Pete was in his element, expounding his ideas with an enthusiasm that was catching.

The young architect had been a lucky find, kicking his heels in frustration in the drawing office of Statham Holdings. He had been just about ready to throw in his resignation and try his luck in York or Leeds when he had discovered to his delight that his new boss was interested in what he had to say.

With everyone's attention engaged, it was the perfect opportunity to watch Annis as she sipped her coffee.

The room was lit by two large chandeliers above the table, and their soft glow cast a sheen of gold over her smooth ivory skin. There had been times when he was away when he had asked himself if he was painting a more beautiful image in his mind than the reality could live up to.

But the reality was even more beautiful. Those violet-blue eyes sparkled with amusement, that soft pink mouth was just asking to be kissed.

He liked the way she had done her hair tonight, with that honey-coloured wave tumbling loose over one shoulder – tempting him to run his fingers through its silken length, to wind it around his hand as he tipped her head back to arch her body hard against his… to trace hot kisses down the delicate curve of her throat… to slip the narrow strap of that elegant black dress back over her shoulder…

Along the table, Annis could feel herself trapped in the hypnotic spell of Theo Lander's dark, level gaze. It was a struggle to breathe; she could almost feel him touching her, slowly stripping her naked, stroking his strong hands across her aching breasts, down over her smooth stomach…

With an effort of will she pulled herself back to reality. "Why don't we take ourselves out onto the terrace?" she suggested brightly. "It might be a little cooler out there."

There was a general murmur of assent as everyone topped up their wine-glasses and carried them outside.

The terrace was a lovely place to sit in the evening. Small clumps of fragrant sedum and thyme crept up between the old flag-stones underfoot, long trails of blossoms hung down from the wisteria which grew along the length of the house.

But tonight it was no cooler than indoors. The air was still, oppressive. Even the moon looked unnatural, glowing a heavy yellow as it ducked and dodged behind swift-moving puffs of inky clouds. "Looks like we may finally get that thunderstorm tonight," Vicky remarked to Annis.

Annis nodded. "The horses certainly seem to think it's coming – they've been fidgety all afternoon. I've brought some of the more nervous ones into their stables, but the rest will probably be happier staying out in the paddock."

"It was a lovely meal – and the company was quite entertaining!" Vicky's eyes danced with mischief as she glanced back over her shoulder. "A few people trying to ease their troubled consciences. As I recall, they were pretty quick to condemn poor Tom Lander at the time - now they're falling over themselves to suck up to Theo."

Annis smiled in agreement, glancing across the terrace to where he had been cornered by Gerald Trenchard and Dennis Forsyth, both key figures on the Planning Committee. Well, that was what he had wanted, she reflected with a touch of sardonic amusement – she could only hope that he was enjoying himself.

As if he sensed her gaze, his eyes turned towards her, glittering darkly in the light of the lanterns dotted around the terrace. In spite of the heat of the evening, which had everyone else wilting, somehow he managed to look utterly cool and relaxed.

His one concession to the temperature had been to discard his jacket and tie, leaving his shirt unfastened at the throat, the cuffs rolled back over his strong forearms. The crisp white cotton seemed to emphasise the width of his shoulders, the lean taper of his torso.

He walked slowly towards her, holding her captive with that mesmerising gaze, slowly unfastening his shirt and shrugging it off. The golden glow of the lanterns gleamed on his sun-bronzed skin, casting shadows across that wide chest and down over the hard-muscled ridges of his abdomen…

She drew in a sharp breath, almost dizzy from the fevered fantasy that had swirled so suddenly into her brain.

With an effort of will she turned her gaze from his, moving across the terrace to speak to some of her other guests – though she could still feel those dark eyes watching her, like a pin-prick of laser light searing into the back of her neck.

"…so he had to run all the way back across the field, in one Wellington boot, with a dozen angry cows at his heels!" A burst of laughter from those around her warned Annis that she had completely missed Jeremy's yarn. She joined in a little belatedly, hoping no-one would notice her distraction.

If they did, she would blame the heat. Her hands felt sticky, and a small bead of sweat was trickling down between her breasts. She moved her shoulders, vainly trying to ease the tension in her spine.

If anything, the night was getting hotter. Not a puff of air was moving; the leaves on the trees down by the river were still. Even the birds had stopped singing. Ominous dark clouds were eating up the stars as they rolled in low across the horizon, and a sharp scent in the air, a metallic zing, warned that the storm was getting close.

It seemed that everyone else shared the same thought. People were getting ready to leave, glancing up anxiously at the sky, hurrying to make it home before the heavens opened.

Annis saw them to the front door, bidding them goodnight in a melee of air-kisses and congratulations on the lovely meal.

"You must give me the recipe for that mushroom sauce – it was delicious."

"Goodnight – have a safe journey."

Pete was one of the last to go. He was absorbed in conversation with one of the other guests about the technicalities of ground-source heating, but he managed to break off long enough to be polite to his hostess.

"Goodnight, Annis. Thank you for inviting me."

"Thank you for coming."

He gazed around the lofty hall, apparently entranced. "It's a lovely house. Early Victorian, isn't it?"

"Mid-Victorian. 1850s, I think."

"That wood panelling is wonderful. Is it original?"

"Yes it is."

"Goodnight, Pete," Theo prompted, gently steering him towards the door.

Annis could feel herself wanting to giggle at Theo's evident frustration as he tried to get rid of the young architect. Of course, once he was gone…

"And the staircase…"

"Yes, the staircase is very nice too," Theo assured him, his guiding hand rather firmer now.

"I'd really love to have the chance to look over…"

"I'm sure Annis would be delighted to show you around. Another time." At last Theo managed to usher him out and close the door. He leaned back against it, those dark eyes glinting with an intent she couldn't misread. "I thought he'd never go."

Annis laughed a little unsteadily. The air between them seemed to crackle with an electric charge, and it was difficult to breathe.

"So," he murmured, huskily soft. "Did you miss me?"

"Oh, have you been away?" She was trying for an air of casual humour, though her stomach was twisting in knots.

"You missed me." He was moving towards her, slowly, smiling like a panther stalking his prey.

"I've been very busy." Her mouth felt suddenly dry, and unconsciously she ran the tip of her tongue over her lips. "It's been so hot…"

He laughed, shaking his head. "Tell me you missed me," he insisted, his eyes glinting with dark intent as he moved closer.

"Heavens, it must be getting late." The tension spiked, and she took a step backwards, to find herself blocked by the banister of the staircase. "I'll just clear the…"

"Whatever it is, it can wait." With a low growl he caught her in his arms. "But I won't. I've been thinking about this moment the whole time I've been away – being alone with you, nothing to disturb us, and the whole night ahead of us…"

The whole night…

She was caught in his spell, helpless as he dragged her supple body hard against his. She had no defence as his mouth came down to claim hers in a kiss of tender possessiveness which seemed to plunder her very soul.

This wasn't the cool, contained Theo Lander she had known for the past few weeks - this was a man who was fuelled by the same primitive forces that were firing her own blood. She could only surrender as his lips crushed hers apart – she couldn't think of anything but the hunger that was consuming her.

His tongue had swirled deep into her mouth in a flagrantly sensual exploration. She lifted herself on tiptoe, her arms wrapped around his neck, curving herself against him as his hands slid slowly down the length of her bare back to rest beneath the soft curve of her silk-clad derrière.

The only conscious thought in her mind was that she never wanted to let him go. She wanted to feel herself wrapped up in his strong arms for ever, wanted to breathe that intoxicatingly male scent that was exclusively his, wanted to share the sweet, moist heat of an endless, endless kiss.

Her head tipped dizzily back as she gasped for air, and she realised that he had scooped her off her feet and was carrying her towards the stairs.

She let her fingers tangle in his hair where it curled crisply over the nape of his neck, then dip inside the open collar of his shirt, sliding down to attack the buttons, fumbling them apart so that she could smooth her palm over the hard warmth of his chest – something she had been longing to do for weeks.

"If you keep that up," he warned softly, "we aren't even going to make it as far as the bedroom."

She slanted him a mischievous glance from beneath her lashes, thrilled at the knowledge of the power she had over him. "Who needs the bedroom?"

"Minx."

It was too much - the intensity of their mutual need made it impossible to get any further up the stairs. They tumbled together in a laughing heap barely half-way to the first landing, a helpless bundle of arms and legs.

Wrapping her arms around his neck Annis lifted her face to his, their mouths meeting in another hungry kiss, their tongues swirling languorously around each other. Her insistent hands had pulled apart the rest of his shirt buttons, and tugged it loose so that it fell open across the wide expanse of his chest, sun-bronzed and covered with a smattering of rough, dark curling hair across the hard male muscles. Just as she had imagined it.

At the same time, he had dragged the clips out of her hair and tossed them aside, and slid down the zip of her dress, sliding the narrow straps off her shoulders and drawing down the fabric to expose the ripe creamy swell of her breasts, naked beneath his marauding hands.

She could feel the edge of the stairs digging into her back, but she didn't care. His hands were on her breasts, crushing their firm swell beneath his palms as the tautly sensitised buds of her nipples hardened, rasping against that soft abrasion, sizzling as his strong, sensitive fingers nipped at them, tormenting them with sweet pleasure.

She whimpered in protest as his mouth left hers, but it was only to dust scalding kisses across her trembling eyelids, the racing pulse that beat beneath her temples, and into the delicate shell of her ear. "I can't believe how much I've wanted you. You must have been about fifteen the first time I noticed you."

"Fifteen?" A bubble of laughter rose to her lips. "Surely not. I'd still have been in my school uniform."

"I know." His hand was still caressing her warm breast. "Disgusting of me, lusting after you like that. You used to roll your skirt up around your waist to show off those heavenly legs, and unbutton your shirt so far down it should have been illegal. More than once I skinned my fingers on an engine block because of the way you were distracting me."

"I don't believe you!" Could it really be true? "You never even noticed me."

"Oh, I noticed you all right. And what I was thinking every time you walked down the street past my dad's place would have got me arrested. It's been a very long wait." He shifted himself to lie above her, his arms on each side of her trapping her as he held up his weight on his elbows, his hot gaze drifting down hungrily over her half-naked body. "But now you're all grown up, and I have you where I want you. And I have a lot of time to make up for."

The dark intent in his eyes made her shiver in anticipation. She had wanted him too - all those years ago she had gazed at him in secret longing as he had worked in his father's garage, her adolescent hormones stirred by the sight of him in his worn T-shirt, her mind filling with fantasies she had barely understood.

But now she was a full-grown woman - now she could touch, slide her hands inside his shirt and across the firm resilience of his flesh, brush her thumbs across the dark, flat nipples, feel the warning tremor of male arousal simmer through him.

"Careful," he growled. "I don't want it to be over too quickly."

Nor did she, as he bent his head over the ripe, inviting swell of her naked breasts, pertly tipped with taut, pink buds. She arched her back, offering herself to his pleasure, her hands laced into the crisp dark curls at the nape of his neck, watching in delicious anticipation as his moist red tongue lapped out to swirl languorously around one ripe, succulent nipple, rasping over it, tasting its sweetness, blowing a shivering puff of air across it to tease her and then nipping at it lightly with his hard white teeth, before moving to the other breast to treat it to the same wicked delights.

This was more than she had ever dreamed possible. She was losing herself in a world of exquisite sensation - everything but this moment, and what he was doing to her, had slipped far from her mind. And as he took one tender bud into his mouth and began to suckle at it with a deep, pulsing rhythm she heard herself cry out as the sheer animal pleasure flooded her veins.

Somehow she had parted company with her dress – she didn't even recall how or when – leaving her wearing only a tiny scrap of black lace which barely covered the tangle of blonde curls that crowned her thighs. Theo was at her feet, slipping off her strappy black evening sandals.

The dark glint in his eyes was promising her wicked pleasures as he kissed the tips of her toes, one by one, making her giggle with delight. He found a tiny spot behind her ankle that made her shiver with heat, and he laughed softly at her reaction as he kissed his way up the length of her slender legs, tracing a scalding path as she let her head tip dizzily back, closing her eyes, focussing only on that delicious touch.

His fingers had hooked into the lace of her skimpy knickers, and her breath caught in her throat as he drew them slowly down, down… all the way to her ankles, and then tossed them aside.

A small shiver of vulnerability feathered over her soft skin, and she opened her eyes briefly to watch as he let his gaze drift over every slender inch of her, his possessive hand caressing her in a long, slow sweep, savouring every changing texture from the silken smoothness of her thighs, the downy curve of her stomach, the aching swell of her breasts with their puckered pink peaks.

Everything female in her was responding to his insistent male demand. Her body arched beneath him as his hands slid into her hair, caging her skull as his mouth reclaimed hers in a kiss of savage tenderness, stirring the fever in her blood. She was his willing victim, surrendering her body and soul to the same dark seas of passion where her heart had long since drowned.

A small voice in her mind was whispering a stark reminder that he had offered her nothing beyond this moment. Just for tonight they could share this physical pleasure – and maybe for a few nights more… a few weeks… even a few months. But there was no promise of anything more.

So this would have to be enough.

His hand stroked slowly down over her slim thighs again, parting them slightly to seek the sweet, secret folds of crimson velvet hidden beneath their crown of crisp curls. His touch was like magic, exploring deeply within, caressing her with a tender intimacy that made her spine curl in ecstasy. With unerring skill he had found the exquisite focus of all her pleasure, stroking it to a sizzling arousal as a soft cry escaped her lips.

"You like that?" he teased, his warm breath fanning her cheeks.

Her brain was incapable of forming an answer – not that it was necessary. Her body was telling him everything he needed to know.

"You're so beautiful – every lovely naked inch of you." His dark gaze slid down over her, hot and possessive. "I've dreamed about this for weeks - why has it taken us so long to get around to it?"

Annis neither knew nor cared. The past and the future had evaporated like morning mist – there was only this moment as Theo shifted to lie above her, holding his weight from crushing her as he coaxed her thighs wider apart. Their bodies seemed to fit together like two halves of one mould, perfectly aligned, made for each other.

He took her with a long, deep thrust, filling needs she had never known existed. She opened her eyes to gaze up at him, all her unspoken love brimming over in her heart.

She clung to him, moving instinctively beneath him, responding to the primeval rhythm he set, the two of them united in a dance as old as time - first slow and grinding then fast and hard, their breathing ragged and their hearts pounding together, their bodies slicked with sweat.

Waves of pleasure were flooding through her like molten gold, heating her blood as if she had a fever. A dark, swirling vortex had caught them up, lifting them higher and impossibly higher, to sweet pinnacles of pleasure, soaring in the flames, until she felt as if she was exploding in a cascade of incandescent sparks, tumbling and spinning through endless space to collapse at last in a tangled heap of arms and legs, sprawled across the stairs.

CHAPTER TEN

IT WAS a long time before Annis felt her heart-beat return to normal. She lay in the crook of Theo's arm, her cheek resting against his warm chest, as her breathing returned slowly to normal. If she could have just one wish, it would be that the world could stand still at this moment, that she could stay for ever in this single point in time.

"So it was true." With a gentle touch he stroked a stray coil of hair back from her forehead. "Your first orgasm."

She lowered her lashes, a blush of pink rising to her cheeks. "How did you know?"

"The look on your face. Surprise. There was no mistaking it." He laughed softly. "There'll be more."

Yes, but how many?

She wasn't going to say it, not out loud. She barely even dared to whisper it deep in her heart: *I love you.* She really wasn't familiar with the etiquette for this kind of situation, but she was pretty sure that it was far too soon to say those words – if it would ever be right.

That thought broke through the web of fantasy she had been spinning in an effort to hold reality at bay. He had made it clear from the beginning. He wanted a mistress – he had offered nothing more than that. Her dreams of love, commitment, a future together… all that would have to remain in the realm of far beyond. A mistress had to be content with the limitations of her role.

Suddenly she felt awkward, lying there naked in his arms – and far too vulnerable. She needed an excuse to…

The excuse came before she had even framed the thought – a resounding crash that seemed to come from somewhere just above the roof.

"Oh no!"

"Annis?" Theo reached for her hand as she scrambled to her feet, but she snatched it free as a second crash sounded, rumbling across the sky. Thunder. "What's wrong?" he asked urgently. "Are you afraid of the storm?"

"No." She looked around wildly for her dress, snatching it up and throwing it on over her head, wriggling as she struggled to zip it up. "It's the horses. I'm sorry – I have to... Please let yourself out. Goodnight."

Annis was off down the stairs as Theo's mind skidded to catch up with the sudden swerve of events. He wasn't accustomed to young women leaping up with a cry of horror when he had just made love to them, and racing off without even bothering to pick up their underwear!

He shrugged into his shirt and zipped up his trousers, bounding down the stairs after her, snatching up his jacket as he went. She had really put him in his place – and she hadn't even realised it!

And now – did she really expect him to just go, leaving her to cope alone with whatever was going on?

She had raced through the kitchen to some kind of scullery, pausing at the back door just long enough to drag on a pair of Wellington boots – gloriously incongruous with that elegant evening dress. As he moved to follow her, the lights abruptly went out, plunging the room into darkness.

Stumbling into a chair, he cursed under his breath, rubbing his shin. A jagged streak of lightening showed him Annis running across a cobbled yard towards a wooden gate in an old brick wall.

As he pushed through the gate behind her another spectacular flash forked across the sky, showing him a stark white image of a large stable-yard. In less than a second the thunder crashed, almost overhead - and all hell seemed to break loose. Horses were whinnying all around him, some kicking at their stable doors in panic.

Dammit - how many horses did she have?

The rain began to fall in a drenching curtain, making it difficult to see. Where was Annis? The flickering orange glow of a storm lamp in one of the loose-boxes caught his eye, and he splashed across the yard, his jacket over his head. She was inside the loose-box, the bottom half of the door bolted behind her.

And as he moved closer, his blood chilled.

The horse was silver-grey, and he was big. He was snorting and squealing, stamping his hooves and shaking his head, his lips drawn back over a dangerous-looking set of teeth, his eyes showing white with terror.

And Annis stood there beside him, quite calm and still, her wet hair plastered against her head, her hand resting on that quivering neck.

He drew in a sharp gasp of horror, but she silenced him instantly, holding up an imperious hand to warn him to stay back. She didn't turn - all her attention was focused on the horse.

Every protective male instinct was urging him to drag her forcibly out of there. But not only would she not thank him for it, he realised immediately that she knew exactly what she was doing. She was talking quietly to the horse – and it was working.

"It's all right – nothing's going to hurt you. I'm here now – you're quite safe."

He watched, fascinated. The horse was clearly terrified of the thunder. He was still trembling, but that soft voice was working a kind of magic. Another slash of lightning strobe-lit the yard with its stark white light, followed almost instantly by another rolling crescendo of sound, but the horse dipped his head, laying it trustingly against Annis's shoulder.

"Poor Silver - you don't like the horrid noise, do you?" she murmured. "There – that's better. There's nothing to be afraid of."

"Why is he so nervous?" Theo asked quietly.

"I don't know." She spared him a quick glance, but her concentration was all on the horse. "I think he must have been ill-treated. He was certainly neglected - he had a dreadful chest infection when he first arrived. He's been here nearly six months now, and it's taken most of that time to settle him. I was worried that the storm would scare him so much we'd be right back to square one again."

"You've adopted him?"

"Temporarily. I hope we'll be able to find a home for him

146

one day. He was picked up by the RSPCA, and the local Horse Rescue Society homed him with me. That's where most of them came from."

"How many are there?"

"Nine at the moment – six horses and three donkeys. We rehomed a couple recently, but we might be getting another one in next week."

"They're all rescues?" He glanced back over his shoulder at the cobbled yard. There were half-a-dozen loose boxes along each side, several of them apparently occupied.

"Yes."

"Why didn't you tell me?"

"I… thought it would put you in an even stronger position." She pushed a wet strand of hair from her eyes. "It would just give you something else to hold over me."

"Did you really think I was such a bastard as that?" he protested, quietly angry - with her, with himself. "No, don't answer that." He held up his hand, a note of wry amusement in his voice. "I probably gave you plenty of reason to think so. All that phoney mistress thing… It was really just a game, a way to get you to spend time with me. We hadn't got off to the best start."

She stared at him for a moment, then began to laugh, those violet-blue eyes dancing with merriment. "So - you thought I was a spoiled little Daddy's girl, and I thought you were a ruthless bastard. It's certainly taken us a while to sort that one out…"

There was another violent crash of thunder, so loud that it startled them both – and they had had no warning, the lightning had flashed at the same instant. This time the crashing continued, closer to hand, and the big horse whinnied in fear, trying to back himself into the far corner of the stall.

"That sounded like a tree coming down," Theo remarked sharply.

"It could have been the big old hornbeam down in the far meadow - it got struck once before, about five years ago, and I've been half-expecting it to happen again." She glanced back at the grey horse. "I ought to go and check on the other horses."

"I'll do it," he offered at once, tossing his jacket over the door of the next stall – his shirt was already soaked through, he couldn't get any wetter. "You stay here with him."

"Thank you." She smiled at him a little crookedly. "You're soaking wet."

"So are you." He laughed softly. "But you look so damned beautiful like that I could lay you down right here in the hay and ravish you - only it would probably spook the horse."

Her cheeks blushed a delightful shade of pink. "It almost certainly would."

"Later then. After a nice hot bath - or maybe during it." Somehow, in the space of moments, everything had just fallen into place, like a winning line on a slot-machine. Why had it all seemed so complicated? "And then we have something very important to talk about."

"Oh...?" She lifted sparkling violet-blue eyes to his in surprised question.

"Like how we're going to deal with the fact that I'm in love with you."

Annis stared after him as he plunged out into the rain.

In love with her? Had he really said that? Or was he drunk? It didn't seem likely - she had never once seen him the worse for drink. But then if he could think she looked beautiful at the moment, with her hair hanging in sodden rats tails around her head and her dress soaking wet and plastered to her skin, sagging at the hem and dripping rain onto the floor, he could only be drunk!

Another flash of lightning sparked across the sky, and she stroked Silver's neck reassuringly. A few second's interval this time before the roll of the thunder suggested that the storm was passing over. Did the rain seem a little lighter? Silver was quieter now, and she sighed with relief - it could have been a whole lot worse.

She turned as Theo came splashing back - and frowned

at the worried expression on his face.

"The horses down in that field at the end look OK – half the tree's come down, but it doesn't seem to have done any harm. But I think you'd better come and take a look at the horse in the big stable just along here. It doesn't look too happy – it's pacing around, and it keeps lying down and getting up again."

"Oh my goodness, that's Amber – don't say she's gone into labour!"

"Well, I wouldn't know what to look for," Theo admitted. "But something's certainly bugging her."

Trying not to convey her sudden anxiety to the big grey, she backed smoothly out of his stable, pausing only to secure the half-door before hurrying down to Amber's stable with Theo. "Damn! I should have looked in on her first," she cursed herself bitterly. "But Silver was in such a panic..."

"Don't beat yourself up over it. The big lad needed you too."

She slanted him a swift smile of thanks, then held up the storm-lamp to get a look into Amber's stable. The bay mare had lain down on the straw now, turning her head along her sweating flank – one glance confirmed the diagnosis. She was in labour.

Annis let herself into the stable and knelt beside the nervous mother, running a hand over the trembling muscles, feeling for the contractions.

"What can I do?" Theo asked, taking his cue from her in keeping his voice low and quiet.

"Can you try to get hold of Vicky - the vet?"

He nodded, and went to fetch his jacket. "What's the number?"

She recited it for him and he jabbed it into his keypad as she turned her attention back to the sweating mare, lying in the straw, breathing heavily. She could feel the foal - at least it seemed that it was the right way round.

She glanced up as Theo grunted and impatiently shook his head. "The storm's interfering with the signal." He slanted a wry glance down at the quivering mare, lying on her side in the stall. "It looks like we're on our own."

Annis pushed the wet hair out of her eyes, and drew in a long deep breath. Then she nodded decisively. "Well, we'll just have to cope until we can get hold of Vicky."

"What can I do to help?"

They worked together swiftly, sweeping out the stall and throwing down a deeper layer of straw, wrapping the mare's tail in a strip of clean sacking and wiping her down with warm soapy water.

By the time they had finished, the foal's dainty feet had appeared. Annis got another strip of sacking and looped it around the slender fetlocks, then handed the two ends to Theo.

"Just keep a steady strain on it as the foal starts to come out," she instructed him. "Don't pull."

"Right."

She glanced up at him a little uncertainly. He was as wet as she was, his shirt soaked through and plastered against his wide chest, his hair dripping over his forehead. But he didn't seem to mind.

"Thank you," she murmured.

Was this the same man who had sat in her father's office just weeks ago, and coldly announced that he owned everything she had thought was hers?

He smiled down at her, that heart-stopping smile that always took her breath away. "I wouldn't miss this for the world." There was no trace of mockery in voice. It had the ring of sincerity.

The storm seemed to have moved away now, the thunder little more than a distant rumble, though the rain was still drumming on the roof and swishing down the drainpipe into the water-butt outside.

Inside the stable, lit by the soft, flickering flow of the storm-lamp, it was strangely peaceful - even cosy. The only sound was the heavy breathing of the mare, and the crackling of the warm hay as she fidgeted.

"I have something for you."

She glanced up at him in surprise.

"I was going to give it to you earlier, but there wasn't an opportunity. It's in the pocket of my jacket."

Puzzled, she eased carefully to her feet so as not to disturb Amber. He had tossed his jacket over the half-door. When she picked it up, she felt something in the inside pocket – a bulky envelope. She drew it out, eyeing it warily.

"What is it?"

"Open it and see."

She slid her thumb under the flap and tore it open. Inside was a letter. As she unfolded it, she recognized the letter-heading of Theo's lawyer. The words at first seemed to dance on the page. *We have been requested by Mr. Theodor Lander to confirm that the registered charge on the property known as Oakwood Lodge has been rescinded.*

Slowly she lifted her eyes to his. "What does it mean?"

"I've cancelled the mortgage on your house. You don't owe me a penny. It's just a small gesture of thanks."

"*Small?* But…"

"It's nothing compared to the chance of clearing my father's name." His dark eyes glinted with warmth. "That was much more than I had ever looked for."

She stared at the letter again. It wasn't just that he had given her back her home, free of any financial lien. He had given her back her freedom, relinquishing the hold he had had over her. She was no longer forced to act out that charade of being his mistress – though with his father's reputation restored, he no longer needed her to.

Now, if they were together, it would be freely, as equals.

She laughed a little unsteadily. "You have Joan to thank really – my housekeeper. She was so sure your Dad was innocent, and I… Well, I remembered what a nice man he was. He fixed my bicycle for me once, when I was little – the chain had come off. He saw me wheeling it down the street, crying, and he called me over to the garage. He fixed it for me right away, and he gave me a chocolate biscuit. Somehow I couldn't believe he could be a criminal, no matter what."

"So how did you find out the truth?"

"I started thinking about that woman you told me about.

My father… He had a string of mistresses. He never made much of a secret about it." Her voice was laced with bitterness. "My mother always knew – he never cared how much he hurt her. I just began to wonder whether the woman could have been one of them. She sounded like his type. It was just a process of elimination, really."

"How did you find her?"

"I didn't – it was Sandy, the journalist who wrote the story. The gist of it is in the paper. The affair lasted for about a year, but she knew my father would never leave my mother for her. So when her husband was offered a transfer to London she decided to go with him, give her marriage another chance."

"Do you think she was telling the truth about not knowing why he wanted her to take the car in for a re-spray?"

"I don't think she knew everything - I don't think she wanted to know. It was a few weeks after she'd moved down to London. He got in touch, and asked her for a 'little favour.' He hinted that if she didn't oblige, her husband would find out about the affair. Although ironically, they split up six months later anyway."

Theo laughed without humour. "I'm not going to feel sorry for her."

"No, I don't suppose you will."

"And your Uncle?"

"I suppose he thought he could bluff it out, as usual. But since the story first broke there have been quite a few more things that have come out of the woodwork. Even if he doesn't face criminal charges, he's been forced to resign from the Planning Committee. Which means you should have no problems when your plans come up for discussion."

He nodded. "And how do you feel about that?"

"I'm not going to feel sorry for him." She repeated his own words, her voice grim. "Only… I'd rather he didn't know it was me. Sandy promised she wouldn't tell anyone who gave her the original information."

"Your secret's safe with me." His dark eyes were smiling in a way she had never seen.

Annis felt a hot little shiver down her spine. "Thank you," she murmured, folding the paper in her hand. "I…"

"Hey, I think we're getting some action here," Theo announced suddenly.

Sure enough, the mare was beginning to strain, her flanks heaving as she pushed. The foal's feet were sliding out, followed by the round butt of a nose, still wrapped in its fine white amniotic membrane.

"OK, I think it's time to give her a little help. Start to pull on the sacking - not too hard, just a steady pressure. Come on, sweetie, you can do it." She stroked the mare's trembling flank. "Give it a good push – that's the way."

"It's coming," Theo reported, a lilt of excitement in his voice. "I can see its ears now."

Suddenly there was a rush as the whole of the tiny foal's neck and shoulders appeared, still covered by the membrane, followed by its chest and then the rest of its body and back legs.

"Is it OK?" Theo queried anxiously as Annis knelt over it, carefully tearing away the membrane with her fingers.

"I don't know…"

She picked up a handful of straw and carefully wiped the foal's nostrils. For a few tense seconds she watched it, willing it to start breathing - if it didn't start on its own, she didn't know what to do. Suddenly she saw the little pink tongue move, and heard a soft swish of air.

"Yes!" She leapt to her feet, dancing up and down. "It's breathing. Oh, that's wonderful! That's so wonderful!" And then she burst into tears.

Theo caught her in his arms, and she sobbed against his chest as they watched its mother lift her head to regard it with gentle eyes, and then ease herself gingerly to her feet. She sniffed at the russet-brown baby, nuzzling around its small, perfect head, and then began to lick it clean.

"Should we help?" Theo whispered softly.

Annis shook her head. "No. It's quite warm enough in here - it won't catch a chill. It's best to let her get on with it."

Theo still had his arms around her, and now he dropped

a kiss on the top of her head. "Our first-born."

She looked up at him, her eyes wide.

"Of course, I hope they won't *all* be foals." He smiled down at her. "It would be quite nice to have a couple of the two-legged variety at some point."

"Babies?"

"Yes - our own babies." He drew her closer. "Not that there's any rush just yet – we'll need to get the wedding out of the way first. I suspect that might cause quite an uproar in the town," he added on a low rumble of laughter.

Annis felt as if Ridgely had unexpectedly slipped into the earthquake zone – everything around her seemed to be spinning. A wedding… He really was talking about a wedding…

"We could… always sneak off somewhere and get married quietly," she suggested tremulously.

"No way." That voice would brook no argument. "This is going to be an occasion. The white frock, the bridesmaids, and a carriage drawn by two white horses. Only not that big brute along there," he added, nodding his head in the direction of Silver's stable.

"But he's a sweetie! Well, so long as nothing frightens him."

"I'll take your word for that." He smiled dryly. "He can stand outside the church with flowers in his mane if he wants to, but he's not pulling the carriage."

Annis decided not to argue. She couldn't anyway - not when he was kissing her like that…

When Vicky arrived an hour later she found them both still in the stable, sitting on a bundle of hay, wrapped up in each other's arms as they watched the delicate little foal balancing unsteadily on its four spindly legs, swaying slightly, wearing an expression of puzzled concentration as it tried to work out the basic principles of standing up, while its mother looked on proudly.

The storm had passed, leaving only a steady dripping sound as the gutters emptied into the overflowing water-butt.

As she walked in, the lights flickered and came back on.

"Well," she remarked, glancing from them to the foal and back again. "You two look as if you've had quite a night!"

DEAR READER

Hi – I hope you've enjoyed reading about Annis and Theo's summer romance as much as I enjoyed writing it. Now may I ask a favour? Please take a moment to go back to Amazon and leave a quick review. I'd really love to know what you think of the story – what did you like about the characters, did you like the setting? Here is the link: **getBook.at/SS-SMC**

If you liked this book, come over to my website and see what else you might enjoy. You can find out more about my books, including those not currently available as ebooks but possibly still in print, from my website:
http://www.susannemccarthy.com

You will also be able to read some of my short stories (not all of them romances) for free.

I'd really appreciate your feedback and reviews. Come and chat with me on Twitter: **@McCarthySusanne** or visit my Facebook page **SusanneMcCarthyX**

CHASING STARS getBook.at/CS-SMC

Kat had a very low opinion of billionaire Javier de Almanzor – and that was before he kept her prisoner aboard his fabulous yacht, the Serenity. Javier was the most sinfully handsome man she had ever seen. He was also a low-life scum-bag.

And she was going to prove it.

Javier was intrigued by the beautiful stowaway. Was she a thief? Or just an honest girl trying to get by in the world as best she could. It would probably be sensible to return her straight to Antibes.

But who needs sensible?

CHAPTER ONE

"HOI - waitress!" The fat man snapped his fingers. "More champagne over here."

"*Say please*," Kat hissed under her breath, fixing a brittle smile in place as she manoeuvred with her silver tray through the elegant throng.

The champagne was flowing like water, the conversation and laughter growing louder by the minute. The crowded saloon was uncomfortably hot, even though the full-length glass doors at the stern had been folded right back to allow the party to spill out onto the wide aft deck.

The golden lights of Antibes sparkled above the marina, rivalling the stars spread across the dark Mediterranean sky.

It was quite a party. If she'd been into celebrity spotting she could have filled a book – seriously A-list movie stars here for the film festival, world-shaking financial moguls, even a smattering of European royalty and a few Arab princes.

There were more diamonds than Van Cleef and Arpels, more gold than Fort Knox, and the rock band playing for the dancers on the lower deck had just had their third number one album.

But even more spectacular than the guest list was the yacht itself – the Serenity, one of the largest in the world. One hundred and thirty-five metres of elegant white hull, with a graceful superstructure and six decks, all gleaming pale wood and opulent suede upholstery, bronzed glass and fabulous displays of exotic flowers, and every luxury a billionaire's money could buy.

Ah yes, the billionaire; Javier Francisco Manuel Thiago de Iñiguez y Almanzor. She had done her research thoroughly, poring over the internet for hours.

There had been plenty to read – on both the financial pages and the gossip sheets.

His father was a wealthy Spanish landowner, his mother a half-French, half-Lebanese former super-model. He spoke nine languages fluently, including Arabic and Russian.

By the age of twenty-two he had exploited that skill to establish himself as a broker in the international oil trade, and now, little more than a decade later, he was reputed to be one of the richest men on the planet.

And one of the most eligible. Watching him covertly from across the room, she was forced to admit that he had the looks to go with his playboy reputation.

He really was extraordinarily handsome, with those angled cheekbones and strongly-carved jaw. He was tall – surely several inches above six feet – and the cut of his black dinner-jacket emphasised the powerful width of his shoulders, but he wore it with an air of casual unconcern which underplayed the expensive tailoring.

He held his proud dark head at an imperious angle, like a hawk - an impression heightened by the perceptive glint in those dark eyes.

She had caught a close-up glimpse of those eyes as she had passed him at the foot of the steps up from the galley earlier in the evening, and been struck by their colour – the rich, dark brown of espresso coffee, with topaz flecks, and thick black lashes which on a woman she would have been inclined to dismiss as fake.

He was also a sleazy, low-life scum-bag. And she was going to prove it.

It was hot. Javier took a small sip of the mineral water in his glass, listening to several of the conversations going on around him.

Were the clocks on strike? The last time he had glanced at his watch – an ostentatious diamond-encrusted monstrosity that he hardly ever wore - must have been at least an hour ago, but the hands had moved barely ten minutes.

A bone-deep ennui seemed to have settled over him as he cast a jaded eye around the crowded saloon. *It's work*, he had to remind himself – not for the first time. If he was doing this for pleasure, he'd probably have thrown himself overboard by now.

In those terms, at least, it had been a resounding success, he acknowledged coolly. No-one turned down an invitation to one of his legendary parties aboard the Serenity.

Like a puppet-master he had gathered many of the richest and most powerful men in the world to drink his champagne and talk business.

There were few people who could bring together Baron Leopold Von Henning, the reclusive German industrialist, and Prince Abdul Mansour, in the same room as three top Hollywood film producers.

The luscious blonde at his side was insistently demanding his attention, flashing her doe eyes at him in unmistakable invitation – an invitation he would probably have declined, even if her husband hadn't been somewhere on the boat, probably issuing a similar invitation to some other nubile young beauty.

"If you don't like your hairdresser, why don't you simply go somewhere else?" he enquired dryly – he knew it wasn't the required response, but he was distracted.

Across the room he had spotted the girl again.

He wasn't quite sure what it was about her that intrigued him. He didn't usually pay much attention to the efficient staff who served him – although he hoped he was never rude.

Even when they owned a pair of legs that could start a riot - he had caught a thoroughly enjoyable glimpse of them when she had been climbing the aft staircase earlier, precariously balancing a laden tray of champagne glasses.

It was the uniform which jarred; it apparently belonged to someone a little plumper and considerably shorter than her. The top-flight catering agency he always engaged to supplement his own crew for on-board events in Antibes and Cannes usually ensured that their staff were immaculately turned out. And they were usually extremely skilful at manoeuvring through a crowd as if almost invisible.

And they didn't usually pull faces at his guests behind their backs.

He had almost laughed aloud at the searing look she had slanted at that unpleasant sleaze-bag Sir Peter

Drummond-Smythe and his equally obnoxious cronies –
particularly when one of them had squeezed her neat derriere.
He had thought for a moment that she was going to deposit
the contents of her tray down the front of his shirt.

But she had returned him a saccharine smile and adroitly
moved away – and then poked out the tip of her pretty pink
tongue at him when she had thought no-one was looking.

She was quite striking to look at. He had noticed earlier
that she was wearing flat shoes – rather worn espadrilles. In
an attempt to diminish her height, make herself a little less
conspicuous?

It was never going to work. The graceful way she moved
would always draw attention, and so would that mop of bright
copper curls - she had bunched them into a knot on top of her
head, but a few corkscrew fronds were escaping to feather
around her face.

Her eyes were the only feature which could be described
as conventionally beautiful – a clear grey-green, and fringed
with long, dark, silken lashes.

In spite of that vivid red hair, her skin was more cream
than pale, with just a light sprinkling of freckles over a rather
pointed nose. And her mouth was way too wide for her face –
though the lips were pink and soft, the colour of wild roses.

But somehow the overall effect was… quirky, and… yes,
beautiful.

In sum - as unconvincing a cocktail waitress as he had
ever seen. With an almost imperceptible flicker of his eyes he
summoned Bob, his head of security, to his side.

"The red-head," he murmured, indicating with a brief nod
of his head.

Bob picked up on her instantly. "I have her. What's the
problem, boss?"

"I'm not sure if there is one. Just a gut feeling. Keep an
eye on her - but be discreet. See if she wanders into any part
of the boat she shouldn't be in, try to find out if she's working
with a partner, even a team."

Bob smiled grimly. "I'm on it."

Javier nodded. If there was anything untoward going on, Bob would discover it. He was ex-SAS, the best in the business – that was why he had hired him, six years ago.

Across the room he watched the girl as she shuffled round a cluster of guests, a small frown of concentration creasing that smooth brow as she precariously balanced her tray of champagne flutes, forgetting to watch out for any guests who wanted to exchange their glasses.

For some reason he found himself hoping that he was wrong – that she was just an innocent, hard-working girl trying to get by in the world as best she could.

He didn't want to think she was a thief.

CHRISTMAS SECRETS getBook.at/XS-SMC

Evie was quite sure there must be all sorts of very good reasons why she shouldn't agree to go into a strange house with a man she didn't know. But she had just crashed her car off a mountain road, and it was snowing heavily.

And just at the moment she couldn't think of any alternative which didn't involve freezing to death.

Alessandro Vitucci had been looking forward to a few day's peace and quiet, a chance to get on with a little work while the rest of the world went crazy over the Christmas season. But he had a feeling that his unexpected guest didn't do peace and quiet.

AND MORE...
Back in the day, I had twenty-five books published by Mills and Boon, and some of them are still available as e-books via my author page on the Mills and Boon website:
http://www.millsandboon.co.uk/susanne-mccarthy

FORSAKING ALL OTHERS
It was love at first sight for Maddy when she met Leo Radcliffe – on the night he got engaged to her best friend.

SECOND CHANCE FOR LOVE
When handsome country vet Tom Quinn rescued Josey, he had little sympathy for her - wasn't she just another spoiled city-girl like his ex-wife?

GROOM BY ARRANGEMENT
Natasha Cole couldn't wait for two years to wrest control of her inheritance from her crooked step-father. But marry Hugh Garratt?

NO PLACE FOR LOVE

*Lacey was **not** having an affair with Sir Clive Fielding. But his arrogant step-son was convinced she was nothing but a gold-digging tramp.*

BAD INFLUENCE getBook.at/BI-SMC
Georgia Geldard was a hard-headed businesswoman with no time for relationships. Least of all with a notorious playboy like Jake Morgan.

PRACTICED DECEIVER
The new Lozier Cosmetics contract was a huge opportunity for model Alysha Jones – but it meant working with Ross Elliot. And that would certainly be dicing with danger.

SATAN'S CONTRACT
Shaun Morgan had inherited the family fortune. Which left Pippa with few options - people's savings and livelihoods were at stake.

DANGEROUS ENTANGLEMENT
Joanna was a serious Egyptologist. And with mining engineer Alex Marshall ready to start blasting for mineral ores close to her excavation, the last thing she needed was any romantic involvement.

Printed in Dunstable, United Kingdom